Dearest Rene —
I love you then
now, and forever —
Your Guy
Dec. 2013

ISBN-13: 978-1492957133
ISBN-10: 1492957135

Printed in the United States of America.

Published November 2013.

ASSUME NOTHING
by J.J. Lenart
A young woman finds a playmate and assumes she has found the man
of her dreams.

THE BULL
by Edgar Brown
An unforgettable adventure for a seven year old.

CROSSING THE LINE
by Edgar Brown
Segregation past but not forgotten.

A DARK AREA
by Prayer Tisdale
Sometimes it takes an angel to get us past the darkest times.

EASY MONEY – HIGH RISKS
by J.J. Lenart
South American grave robbers discover the pitfalls of their business,
the hard way.

FIRST SOLO
by F. Clifton Berry, Jr.
No matter how many flying hours later logged, a pilot's first solo
flight is unforgettable.

A FOLK HERO OF SORTS
by Patricia Boswell Kallman
He was the right man to give us a clue!

FOR EVERYTHING THERE IS A SEASON
by Molly Templar
This poem describes the things we see, hear, smell, taste, and touch
during each season.

GAMBLING
by Richard Katchmark
Most of my overnight business trips are forgettable—not this one.

i

HOW TO SAY GOODBYE IN RUSSIAN
By Denice Jobe
It had been a relief to go to Russia, to outrun grief for a while...

I ALWAYS THOUGHT I WAS A NEW YORKER
by Patricia Boswell Kallman
A woman discovers she is not too old to learn a new truth.

I BRING YOU YOUR WIFE
by Rebecca Thompson
Love. Longing. Mourning. A living wife and a buried husband yearn
for each other.

THE JOB AND THE DEAD
by Rebecca Thompson
A startling and revealing interview with a traffic homicide detective.
The officer describes the pain of grieving families and the personal toll
of handling death on a daily basis.

LILY IN BLUE
by Dana King
A private investigator's case ends when the bill is paid. Some clients
are unforgettable.

LOST SHOE
by Patricia Boswell Kallman
Perspective comes with age!

THE MAGIC FIRE AND OTHER CAMP ADVENTURES
by Ruth Perry
On hot summer nights when the stars are out those unforgettable camp
memories always come beaming back to me.

MY GUERILLA POET
by Rebecca Thompson
A father haunted by the ghosts of his past lives is disconnected from
his children. A daughter discovers poetry is the way to reach him.

POPUP
by John C. Stipa
A troubled father-to-be receives a gift from a father that was.

THE POWER OF LOVE
by Diane Hunter
An act of love and faith forges a bond between a grandfather and his newborn grandson.

RAGS TO RICHES
by Mary Ellen Gavin
RAGS TO RICHES explores the life and changing times of the early 1950s in Chicago.

RED AND WHITE
by Kalyani Kurup
The sheer beauty of that sight was enough to make it unforgettable forever. However, there was also a sequel to the incident that burned the memory of that morning forever in my mind although in a slightly unpleasant way.

TEENAGE UNWISDOM
by Edgar Brown
Youth, guns and judgment.

THE WAGON RACE
by Edgar Brown
A lesson for life.

WALLS
by Hannah Grace Stanton
Words can be among the most effective tools for breaking down walls.

WHAT I DID FOR LOVE
by Sunny Hersh
When you're nineteen and in love, taking big risks can seem like the safest thing to do.

ASSUME NOTHING

By J. J. Lenart

What do smart people say about the word 'assume'? They say to never use it. It makes an ASS out of U . . . and of ME.

I don't consider myself a paranoid naysayer. Nevertheless, I try to never assume anything. That's why the first objective on my list of 'Things To Do' when I returned to Washington, D.C. was to drag my weary body to where my employer's offices were located on K Street and ensure I still had a job. I figured if the American Petroleum Institute still wanted me after doing their grunt work in Venezuela for the past three years, it would be safe to find a place and settle down. But I wouldn't assume that as a fact . . . I'd check first.

* * *

The seventh thing on my 'To Do' list was to find Sara Miller. Sara and I had never dated, as in the romantic context. We preferred to call ourselves snuggle-bunnies. We provided each other with a mutual safe-haven from the rigors, ups-and-downs, and disappointments of finding true love. Except I had recently heard from a close mutual friend that dear sweet Sara had gotten herself married, and I couldn't wait to find her and tell her how happy I was for her. As a righteous aside, I also wanted to check out the lucky guy, as if he needed my seal-of-approval for taking my sweet Sara's hand in marriage.

It took fourteen calls, but I finally found her . . . or, at least a phone number where she was supposed to be. It's amazing how easy it is to get lost after three years.

"Hello?" a strange voice greeted me over the line.

"Hi. This is Jack Stewart. Is this the home of the former Sara Miller?"

"Jack?" The voice seemed to recognize my name, anyway. "Is that really you?"

"In the flesh. And I'm back in D.C. Who is this?"

"It's me, Jack. Trish. Sara's sister."

An image flashed across my mind. "Trish! Thank God. I was afraid I had another bad number. You have no idea how hard it's been finding you or anybody else in the family. Is Sara there?"

"Sorry to say, but she's not here at the moment. She had a late doctor's appointment, but she should be back in about an hour."

"She okay?" I asked in what I hoped sounded like a sincere tone, because I always did care for Sara. Probably even loved her, truth be told. "Nothing's wrong. Right?"

"Nothing that a pill can't fix," Trish told me.

Well, I had found her and she was okay. "Look, tell her I called. I'll try back in . . ."

"I have an idea," the younger sister interrupted me. "Why don't you just come over and surprise her when she gets home. If she phones beforehand I won't even tell her you called."

I considered the suggestion for a fleeting moment. What the hell! I thought. Why not? It would be great to see her again. I had nothing going on that evening, anyway.

"You there, Jack?" Sis asked when I didn't answer soon enough.

"Yeah. I'm still here, Trish. You sure I won't be interrupting anything? What if she comes home with the man-of-the-house? I don't want to create an uncomfortable situation."

"Trust me, Jack. Jean-Pierre won't be here with her."

"Jean-Pierre? Is that his name? I heard he was Swiss."

"That's his name and he is Swiss," she confirmed, "but his family is French. It's a bit complicated, Jack. Sara can tell you all about it."

"Okay," I said, thinking Trish sounded a bit odd when talking about her brother-in-law. "I'll do it. I'm at Clyde's in Georgetown. Where is she living?"

"Arlington . . . right across the Potomac and up Wilson Boulevard."

"No problem. I can be there in fifteen minutes."

"Excellent. Got a pen? I'll give you the address."

* * *

The short cab ride took almost thirty minutes. The delay was caused by the crazy D.C. rush-hour traffic and a quick stop for a few bottles of wine.

The address was an upscale apartment building about a half-mile from the Rosslyn Metro stop, one of the busiest subway interchanges in the area. I didn't want to lose my cab, so I used my cell phone and called the apartment from the car once it was outside her building's entrance. No sense in having to wait for another ride if no one was home.

"Hello?" the distinctive throaty-sweet voice answered.

"Hey there, snuggle-bunny," I tried my softest seductive voice. "It's been a long time. Wanna fool around?"

"Jack?" she asked hesitantly, as if wondering if she'd heard right. "Is that really you, Jack?" and I sensed she was on the verge of tears.

"In the flesh."

"Where are you?" she blurted before I could say more.

"In a cab," I told her, "in front of your apartment building."

"Oh, God! Please come up here, Jack!" she gushed through sputtering sobs. "Please come up here, fast."

"Right away," and I broke the connection.

* * *

The man at the front desk waved me past the entry foyer as if my arrival had been expected. Surprising me, when the elevator door opened, Trish was aboard and hurried off and gave me a quick, limp, Raggedy Ann hug. "Thanks for coming, Jack," she whispered, and then pushed herself away. No smile, no kiss on the cheek. No kiss anywhere.

"Hey. No problem. What's going on? Are you my escort to the honeymoon suite?" I tried joking.

She gave me a weak smile, but that was all. "Maybe another time. Right now I've got a date and I'm late. It'll give you guys time to talk for as long as you like."

"Oh. Okay. But don't rush off on my account. I just wanted to congratulate the bride. Guess I missed out on another of the good ones, huh?"

"Yeah. Right," and she darted off as a yellow cab appeared

3

outside the wall of glass windows and the set of double doors.

* * *

I had an odd premonition during the elevator ride to the eighth floor. It wasn't necessarily that something seemed strange, it was more like something just didn't feel right. And I wondered what I might be walking into with my barely-announced arrival. It couldn't possibly be an irritated husband.

I didn't have long to wait.

I found Sara's apartment easily enough but, before I could reach for the tiny knocker by the peephole, the door swung open and my old friend lunged at me like I was a life jacket on a sinking ship. All I could see she was wearing was a ratty old robe.

"Oh, Jack!" she wailed past my ear.

"What . . . ?" I started to say, but her hysterical sobbing drowned out my question, and I suddenly needed both hands to handle my old friend's clutching body as well as to catch my balance. One of the few times Sara's five-foot-eight stature proved to be a burden.

The paper bag in my left hand fell with an audible crash of broken glass and I immediately knew that at least one of the three bottles had broken. Damn! I thought, don't be the liter of red.

"Jack! Jack!" she stuttered. "What am I going to do, Jack?" the full sentence finally came out.

What the hell was she talking about? I wondered. "Well, for openers," I said, hoping to bring a focus to the real problem at hand. "I think we should clean up the mess I just made on your foyer floor." The pungent scent of red wine started to invade the small space.

"Huh?"

"You know . . . before it ruins the carpet."

"Oh."

At least she stopped crying for a moment. "I brought wine, baby, to celebrate our reunion." For some reason it suddenly seemed like a better reason to toast that than her recent nuptials.

"Oh," and she broke her embrace to see the mess spreading away from the soggy, burgundy blotch on the large paper bag.

"Sorry about the accident," I said. "I've never been missed that much by anyone before."

She smiled and looked at me sheepishly . . . as if she was

4

drugged, drunk, or both.

"Why don't we clean this up first and then we can spill the rest of the wine in a more civilized manner."

Sara smiled at the old quip. "Okay," and she sniffled before dabbing at her nose with a crumpled Kleenex clutched tight in her left hand.

Years past, we used to call each other with an invitation to 'spill wine' together. The awkward grin of recognition didn't do much to mask her red-ringed eyes or the brighter red nose, though. She looked terrible.

I rescued the two undamaged bottles of white before I did any tidying up, and cleaned them off in the galley kitchen sink. Once that was done, I worked on the spill and removed the broken bottle pieces from the foyer floor, happy that the small area rug didn't get a drop splattered on it. Nothing on my shoes or the legs of my slacks, either. Good. Trashing a new suit wasn't in my plans. The few stray splashes of burgundy that did escape all managed to land on the baseboard and were easily wiped up with a damp cloth.

While I toiled with my mess, Sara changed clothes. The entire scenario reminded me of so many other times we had spent together in the past. Made no difference who made the mess — Sara, or me, or both of us — I was usually the one left on my knees with a wet cloth, while sweet Sara freshened up. Maybe it was her way of washing away the associated guilt because, as I recalled further, there was more than one occasion where a pang of guilt might have been involved.

A half-hour later, I had the spill cleaned, the bright lights flipped off and replaced by a few small-wattage lamps, and a soft nest of pillows and throws piled on the lone living room couch. A modular stereo set-up played soft jazz at a micro-volume. A similar setup to days long gone when we'd gripe and whine into late-night hours.

"Ready when you are, princess!" I shouted past my seat.

When she reemerged from the bedroom, I had just put down a bottle of white wine, still half full. Two glasses were on the coffee table.

"Think you're ready, huh?" she asked past sniffles and a fresh tissue.

"Come on over here and tell me everything," I invited her. "It can't be that bad."

5

"Says who?" she hiccupped past a shiver.

"You got your health, right?" I asked playfully. "All the parts working the way they're supposed to?"

That made her smile . . . or, cough and smile . . . before she blew her nose again. "Yeah, Jack. I'm healthy," and she settled into her end of the soft couch tucked under a knitted throw.

"Sex still good?"

That's when she kicked me from under the covers.

I feigned being struck in the groin and doubled-over, groaning as if in excruciating pain.

"Oh, Jack! I'm so sorry," and she put her glass back on the table before reaching a comforting hand to me.

I looked ever so slightly to see the worried, caring look on her face, then kissed her hand.

That was when she swatted me on the top of the head. "You fake," she spit.

"Hey! You kicked!"

"I missed!" she hissed back.

"But you didn't know that."

"Damn you, Jack. You're still the same," she pretended to be annoyed.

"Exactly the same, snuggle-bunny. So let me make it better," I whispered. "Lean over here and give me some sugar."

And she did, but the lingering 'welcome home' kiss turned out to be much sloppier than any we had ever shared before. Probably because of all the tears that were mixed in with the embrace.

* * *

Sara and I talked for the next five hours . . . mostly about her and what she'd been up to. The predominant subject concerned her husband, a smooth player named Jean-Pierre Tournôt.

It seems Sara met the thirty-two-year-old Swiss banker while on a week-long business trip to Bermuda nineteen months earlier. Both were doing a lot of traveling to Caribbean islands, so they managed to hook up at least three times a month for almost half-a-year.

The guy was handsome, a great dresser, well-educated with a promising career, and fun. While they vacationed and played, Sara and Jean-Pierre tried it all. Gambling. Snorkeling. Scuba diving. Parasailing. Wind surfing. And when in Europe, skiing all over the Alps. The traveling had been great. The partying had been better. And the sex had been better than better.

"Dammit, Jack, I assumed this was the real deal. How could I have been so stupid?"

No reason for an answer here. It was a rhetorical question, for certain. Anyway, she'd said the word, not me. She assumed! But who was I to lecture her anyway. . . especially now?

So she went on and on, *ad nauseam*, and the time ticked away just like the wine.

The families had met and gotten along fabulously. Everything seemed better than anyone could want or expect. All was so good, in fact, that a mid-July wedding had been staged. A big wedding, too, with almost two hundred invitations sent out . . . of which eighty went to European attendees.

All but four showed up for the event. A husband-and-wife team who were U.S. Army officers and out of the country, and me and my date. Damn! But I didn't know. I was in Venezuela doing rot-gut oil exploration in the soggy, buggy rain forest.

So what was the problem? I wondered. These tears sure weren't because I missed the big show.

Was good ol' Jean-Pierre a pedophile? A serial killer? A molester? Some other form of deviant felon on-the-run? Or was Mr. Perfect terminally Ill? What was it that had burst dear sweet Sara's bubble?

"So what happened?" I couldn't refrain from asking any longer.

"I need more wine, first," she said, and got up to return with two freshly opened bottles. This time both were red.

"Sara, honey, I'm not sure it's a good idea to keep tossing down this stuff. I've already got a decent buzz on."

"Drink or don't drink, Jack," she snapped at me. "I don't care. But I need it at this point."

"Fine," I said . . . whatever 'this point' meant. "But you still need to finish your story before you pass out." God, I hated wine-drunks. Their breath always reeked and they usually made a vile mess sometime in the night.

She took a long swallow and half the full glass disappeared. "You know how much it costs to throw a wedding?"

"No clue," I confessed. "Never thought about it before. Probably lots, knowing the affair your mother would want to put on."

"No kidding," she said before drinking more. "This was supposed to be the wedding of a lifetime."

Uh, oh. She didn't say it, but I caught the important words. 'Was supposed to be', and 'lifetime'.

"The tab for the whole shebang was priced out at eighty thousand dollars," she told me. "That was supposed to cover all of it. Gown. Flowers. Cake. Photographer. The airline tickets. Limos and cars. Hotel rooms. The church. The reception. The rings. The favors. A two-week honeymoon to Australia. And all kinds of piddlin' crap."

"That's a lot," was all I could think to say.

"Jean-Pierre even got me to rent the apartment in Geneva where we were going to live. He said he was too busy. I paid two-months' security fee, and six months in advance. He's been living in it for the past three months."

"Pretty generous," was all I could think of to say.

"Well, it's all for nothing, 'cause the marriage is finished!" and she drained her glass before reaching for the bottle.

Hell, I knew that from what she'd said before. But why?

"And, do you know what that spineless bastard gave me as an excuse to get the marriage annulled?"

"Annulled?"

"Yeah. Annulled," she said before taking a swallow.

I'm sure I had no idea . . . but I did reach for my own glass of wine.

"He said he needed to tend to important family business and it was a bad time for him."

"Meaning important Swiss family business?" I quizzed her.

"Hell, I don't know," she confessed before emptying her glass. "I was so shocked at what he said I never thought to ask. And, I had all the reason to get in his face, too . . . but he did it over the phone with a bad international connection."

"That was it?"

"I told him I understood," she said in a soft whiny tone, "and that he should take whatever time he needed to help his family. Some kind of crap like that."

"That's all you said?" I challenged her in disbelief.

"Lame, huh?"

"Then what?" I wanted to hear it all.

"I guess you'd say reality set in when I spoke with my mother and sister."

I'll bet it did, but I didn't say it. I knew Sara's family as well as anyone. Hell, I'd been friends with Sara since before high school, and all through college and grad school. I drank most of my wine and eyed the bottle that was nearly empty.

Sara volunteered: "There was maybe ten thousand dollars we could still get refunded. Most of that was in the photographer's fees."

"Jeez."

"Wait! It gets better," she kept going. "Now I have to return all the gifts. You know, UPS and FedEx them back to the senders. Hell, Jack, the shipping's probably going to cost most of the money I managed to salvage."

"Wait a minute," I interrupted her. "Hold on a second. You mean your family is eating all this expense themselves?"

"Mom and Dad gave me twenty thousand. That was what they had set aside. I came up with the rest."

"You found sixty-thousand dollars of your own money? Where? I may have been gone for a while, but there's no way you stashed away that kind of money after three years' work."

"No kidding!" she spit.

"So where . . . ?"

She cut me off. "My grandmother got a line-of-credit on her property in the country," was the explanation.

"Oh, jeez, Sara," I didn't know what to say. Sara's grandmother was a sweet old lady, but she couldn't afford to be doing that. "What about the guy — your husband — Jean-Pierre — how much had he ponied up for the event?"

"Not a damn nickel!" she growled, and grabbed the last bottle.

* * *

The last thing I remembered before falling asleep in a jumbled mass of pillows and throws on Sara's living room floor . . . with Sara in my arms . . . was something about a 'meeting of the minds' at the Miller homestead in suburban Great Falls.

Fortunately for both of us, the gathering was scheduled three days later on Sunday morning. Brunch was to be served first, and then

9

the four of us would focus on the disaster at hand. Sara's dad, a successful real estate developer, said he'd catch up later after he finished inspecting a few of his projects in the area.

That meant it would be Sara, sister Trish, and Mrs. Miller, who I had known for years as Ellen . . . and me.

* * *

I loved the Miller homestead. A comfortable Spanish-style villa done in stucco with a burnt terra cotta roof on twenty-or-so acres of rolling Northern Virginia countryside. Not obscenely large, but not what anyone would call 'cramped space', either. The estate was entirely enclosed by a white post-and-slat fence. A small stable, sited behind the house and out of sight of gawkers, was home to a half-dozen riding horses. Sara and Trish's.

"Okay," Ellen Miller started as soon as the four of us were settled. "I've got a list I made up. Unless someone has a problem, let's go over that first."

"Fine," Sara murmured in resignation.

Trish and I said nothing. I don't believe anyone expected us to. In fact, at that moment, I wondered what the hell I was even doing there. But, since I'd eaten their food, I guess the least I could do for my struggling friend was stick around and lend support.

"I believe the first thing we need to do is mail the cash gifts back as soon as possible," Mom began. "How are you doing with that, Sara?"

Sara answered without looking up from the surface of the glass-topped table. "I checked the bank, Mom, like you told me to."

"That Swiss bank?"

"Yes. The one where Jean-Pierre insisted we deposit all the gift money."

"How much did you put in?"

"I guess all of it," she answered, her soft voice betraying her defeat, "but it's gone now."

"What? What are you saying? That the account is empty?"

"He took it all but the minimum amount to maintain the account," my friend blubbered.

"What a thoughtful bastard!" the elder woman bristled. "Exactly how much was his last withdrawal?"

10

"Forty-two thousand dollars," Sara told her.

"Forty-two thousand?" Ellen Miller repeated in an incredulous tone.

"Do we have to do this, Mother?" Sara asked, as if pleading for sympathy. "This is so humiliating," and tears started to drip from her downcast eyes.

"Darling, I'm truly sorry about all this. None of us saw it coming. But three weeks have already slipped by, and we have to get a handle on this disaster. What about the material gifts? Did you make the list like I asked you to?"

"Yes," she answered. "Here," and she slid a folded piece of tattered paper toward her mother. "I'm pretty sure I got it all listed."

"What about the actual gifts?" the cross-examination went on. "Do you have them all accounted for?"

"More than half are in Europe," Sara confessed.

"Probably the ones that were the most valuable, too, I imagine."

"Probably," and the tears started seeping in earnest. "Can't we stop for a while. Jack doesn't need to hear all this," and she looked to me as if wishing I'd help stop the pain.

"Jack," Mother Miller looked my way, "do you mind if I cover a few more questions with Sara?"

"Not at all, Ellen," I answered in a soft tone. "I'll stay as long as you like."

"Thank you," and she turned her attention back to my Princess Pal. "I took the time to compose a note to include with each of the gifts we return, Sara. It's very simple and to the point. I suggest we owe this to our friends and family members who contributed to this unintended fiasco."

"Can I read it later?"

"Of course," her mother answered, and she slid the mock-up of the note to her troubled daughter. "One last issue, then."

"What's that?" Sara asked, sounding like she might have found her second breath in this marathon of familial torture.

"Your father and I are curious about the status of you finding an attorney to handle the legal action."

Sara exhaled deeply, as if someone had just hit her in the belly with a medicine ball. "Mr. Jankowitz, Dad's business lawyer, sent me to three people. Two only do interstate divorces, and one handles cases for Catholics with annulments involving The Vatican."

"So where does that leave us?"

"I have another meeting with one of Mr. Jankowitz's junior partners tomorrow."

"Tomorrow, as in this Monday?"

"Yes, mother. Monday. Tomorrow. At nine-thirty."

"I'd like to join you, if you don't mind."

"Fine," Sara murmured, sounding thoroughly defeated.

* * *

Sara wasn't very good company after the session with her mother. She knew it, and I knew it. Regardless of our status as good friends, or whatever, she said she needed some time and space and asked if she could call me later.

"No problem, sweetie," I said before I gave her a bear-sized hug and planted a flat kiss on her forehead. "You've got my cell number and my room number at the Key Bridge Marriott. Whenever you feel like hooking up."

"Thanks, Jack."

* * *

I didn't hear from Sara until Wednesday night. It was after midnight, and I had fallen asleep in my California-king reading an old James Patterson thriller. I'm a big fan of his Alex Cross mysteries.

"Jack?" she started out tentatively.

"Hmmm? That you, baby-girl?"

"I woke you up, didn't I?"

"No," I lied. "I was reading and dozed off, that's all."

"Liar."

"What's up?"

"You remember Sunday?"

"You kidding?" I stalled for focus. "I'll never forget it. Gives a guy a different take on the merits of a wedding involving any more than two people."

The quip made her chuckle.

"Why you asking?"

"Well, I did what you said I should do, and guess what?"

I suddenly felt the need to sit up and put my feet solidly on the floor. If I was about to be named as a co-conspirator, I sure in hell wanted to know what I had done in the first place. "Slow down, sweetheart. First tell me what I said you should do."

"You said I should find out when that louse was out of town and rob the place."

Uh, oh. I remembered, now. "I said that, huh?"

"So, I called the building's concierge . . ."

"In Switzerland?" I cut in.

"Right . . . in Geneva . . . and guess what?" she asked excitedly.

I wasn't sure this would be good, but decided to be her straight man. "Okay. What?"

"Jean-Pierre is gone," she gushed over the phone. "I mean, he left today," she clarified her report, "and he won't be back for ten days."

"You're kidding," it sounded too good to be true.

"No, I'm not Jack. The bastard is gone."

"So now what?" I dared to ask.

"I also checked with *Banque Neuf* over the net and found out the VISA card we applied for is still valid," she gushed with enthusiasm. "They're overnighting me a replacement for the one I mistakenly melted with my curling iron."

"No joke?" I asked with a huge smile on my face.

"So, what do you say?" she went on. "Your passport up-to-date?"

"You really want to do this?"

"Jack, do you remember the time Alex Weston snapped that shot up my gown at graduation?"

The memory actually made me smile wider, causing my jaw muscles to ache. "Oh, yeah. You weren't wearing any underwear, as I recall."

"Piss on you, Jack!" she obviously needed to put me in my place. "You remember how he paid?"

"Jeez, Sara, that was some nasty stuff."

"Precisely."

* * *

13

I didn't see Sara again until we met at the security gate at Dulles International Airport in the rolling Virginia countryside west of D.C. She gave me my ticket, flying coach, while she enjoyed the relative luxuries of first class. She explained it was to maintain the semblance of propriety as she was still a married woman.

That was bull, and I knew it. We were flying separate because she didn't want me to know what she had in store for her slimeball husband, Jean-Pierre Tournôt. If he got a smidgeon of what poor Alex Weston got for daring to humiliate Sara Miller, he'd be happy to be rid of her for life. I couldn't remember all the words to that old cliché about 'a woman scorned', but felt sure at the time it applied to what Sweet Sara had in mind for her man.

The itinerary Sara had arranged, courtesy of Monsieur Tournôt's credit card, was busy, to say the least. Once we landed in London, we took separate planes to Paris. From there, separate planes — again — to Geneva.

A stuffed limo took Sara to the *Grande Suisse Apartment* complex. I showed up a few minutes later, by cab, and she introduced me to the concierge as her brother from the United States. As for all the luggage and cases she had with her, she explained to the elderly gentleman that they held all the gift packages she and Jean-Pierre had received at their wedding.

That was the only time I suspected fake-Sister Sara of having an ulterior motive for asking me to join her on this nefarious outing. She needed reliable, cheap, uncomplaining labor. And, no doubt, that was me! Because it was me who was left with the chore of moving all those awkward bags and heavy boxes from the vestibule to the sixth-floor apartment where she and her absent husband had rented a home with her grandmother's money.

As soon as the door was closed, Sara bee-lined it to the bedroom and opened her suitcase. But it didn't hold much clothing. Maybe two outfits, tops, with coordinated shoes and bags. Otherwise it was filled with work clothes: cut-off jeans, shorts, sweatshirts, t-shirts, socks, and Nike's. Rather than a vacation, it appeared Sara had packed as a traveling cleaning woman.

"Okay," she said as she reappeared in the bedroom doorway, "ready to get started?"

What else could I say? "In for a penny, in for a pound. I'm here, so I might as well pull my share of the load. What have you got cooked up in that devilish mind of yours?"

"First I have to make one connection," she shared a snippet of her still mysterious plan. "Get yourself a beer and rest your feet for a few minutes."

I did as Sara instructed, and even got her one to sip on. Then, I listened in awe as she spoke what I thought was flawless French to at least four different people at the Charles De Gaulle International Airport in Paris. Her aim seemed to be to find someone, somewhere, who could confirm when her errant husband had left the country and when he was booked to return.

Finally hanging up, she looked my way and reported: "He won't be back until next Wednesday. Let's plan on being out of here by Monday."

"Why is it you still amaze me?" I asked her.

She smiled at the question. "Didn't know I could *parlez Francais*, did you, Jack?"

"Nothing like that," I admitted.

That's when she winked at me . . . something she used to do whenever we were involved in mischief . . . and walked up to me and planted a short hard kiss on my lips.

"What now?" I wondered out loud.

"Now we go shopping."

* * *

Up to that point in my life, I had had no clue my dear old friend was capable of such malicious pillage. I guess a humiliating experience like a failed marriage — especially one with a life span measured in days — can do that. It probably helped Sara's twisted motivation that she and her family had taken such a huge financial bathing during the torturous ordeal.

From Saturday night through Monday afternoon, we shopped almost literally until we dropped. We bought anything and everything that Sara saw and liked — not just fine clothes, either. There were watches. Jewelry — gold, silver, platinum, and bejeweled. China. Crystal. Art. Antiques, that I knew nothing about. She even bought me a pair of tailored suits, with all the accoutrements. What a pal. Tens of thousands of dollars worth of all kinds of stuff. All to be packaged and mailed back to the States. VISA to the rescue. Just charge it all!

15

The local upscale restaurants also provided an outlet for the available credit line to be drained. Cash advances also played into her plans. Thousands of U.S. dollars were gathered and stuffed into cases of ill-gained wedding gifts packed for air shipment back to the States. The apartment was pillaged of everything of value . . . even a few of Jean-Pierre's familial heirlooms, for barter later in the final divorce wars expected down the road. In retrospect, we used no fewer than four rolls of bubble-wrap to ensure against later shipping breakage . . . and that was just for the loot packed and taken from the apartment.

The few days we were there were so jam-packed with places to go and larcenous things to do that the hours literally flew past us. It made no difference that we were up at the crack-of-dawn and stayed out until crazy hours in the evening. Sara was on a mission and would not be denied.

And when the credit card limit was reached early on Monday morning, Sara used an outpouring of tears at her husband's bank to get a credit extension. After all, her new husband was a blossoming bank official who had left his bride in a strange land. Wasn't he traveling on the bank's business? Of course he was. So, wasn't it reasonable to expect that the bank would see fit to help her get settled by providing nothing more than more cash? Naturally it was.

So, with our suitcases bulging with new clothes . . . and, with new suitcases stuffed with more clothes and pricey artifacts from her husband's Geneva apartment . . . Sara declared her pillage complete at two o'clock on Monday afternoon. A FedEx truck, with a driver and a four-man team of baggage handlers, hurriedly took all the loot away.

But, if I thought what Sara had done with that joint-use credit card was dastardly enough, I was thoroughly unprepared for her true finale.

As soon as the last of the packers had left, she moved both of our carry-on bags to the home's entry foyer and said: "Jack, take a break, will you?"

"Sure. What's up? I thought we were leaving."

"I just need a few more minutes to savor the moment. Get a beer if you like."

"Okay. But don't be long," I cautioned her. "Remember, we still have a flight to catch."

"Don't worry," and she gave me a lingering kiss on the cheek before heading to the bedroom.

16

I watched a noisy soccer game on the television but, after a second beer, I thought she was taking too much time and went looking for her. What I found was one of the most heinous scenes I had ever witnessed.

There, in the newlywed's bedroom, I found dear sweet Sara — dressed in her most tattered rag cut-offs — completing her farewell message. Her *coup de grâce,* so to speak.

The drapes were sliced to shreds. The wallpaper was carved with irreparable scratches and patches, and all the furniture was marred. The mattress was stabbed and cut, as were all the pillows and chair cushions. I suspected the imposing hammer on the bed was the tool that had been used on the mirrors and the door hardware. Probably drowned out by the noisy soccer game.

As for the rest of it, she had somehow found an industrial sized pump-action spray can and loaded it with Clorox bleach. I could see a pair of gallon jugs by the window, and the room reeked of the caustic vapors. She had systematically doused every shred of wardrobe that her husband owned. The suits that hung in the closets. His shoes. The contents of the drawers. Everything. She even doused the shredded bed linens and draperies, the carpeting, and the walls.

But that wasn't all of it. On top of the pungent corrosive spray, she added a film of spray paint. First red, then black, and finally green. The smell was awful. Just awful . . . but the sight was even worse.

"Isn't the paint a bit of overkill?" I managed to ask.

Sara never slowed down from her chore. "It makes me feel better," was all the explanation I got. Then, as if to dismiss me, she said: "I'll be through here in a few minutes. Why don't you take our bags downstairs and wait in the lobby."

"Want me out of the way, huh?"

She kept spraying. "No need for both of us to get messy," she murmured. "Anyway, I still need to visit the kitchen and the living areas."

Well, at least she knew what she wanted to do, I thought. "Think it will take long? I can always reschedule our flights."

"Won't take long, Jack," was all she answered, "but it might help if you get us a cab and load our stuff."

"Okay. You going to leave the card?"

Sara looked at me with the oddest sneer while she refilled the spray can. "No way, Jack. We're not done yet. We're going to need it when we get to Barbados."

"Oh, yeah. Barbados," and I quietly left to the sharp crashing sounds of china and crystal breaking.

The last look I had of Sara was with the hammer in her hand, headed for the kitchen where all the new stainless-steel appliances were quietly awaiting her final wrath.

* * *

The turboprop out of Geneva departed as scheduled, as did the trans-Atlantic flight from Paris. This time, though, we were both in first class, eating and drinking with an appetite to spare. It had been a rough three days in Switzerland. So much to do, and no time for rest.

First stop en route to the Caribbean and a *bona fide* vacation was Bermuda. We had an unexpected four-hour layover due to a heavy storm moving north in the western Atlantic. Some said it was the first hurricane of the season, but not such a bad one.

To kill time, we wiled away the hours in an airport bar at the airline's expense. "First class tickets will do that for you," Sara explained.

"So, what do you think your husband's reaction is going to be?" I finally asked.

She thought a moment before answering: "Hopefully he'll understand that a speedy divorce is in his best interest. I mean, hell, he's got no recourse since we're still legally married. I can get inside wherever he's living."

"You think you're all squared-up with the guy, now?"

"Hell, no!" she bristled. "But I can live with how it worked out."

"That's good, baby-girl," I said as I leaned back in my recliner, "because I sure don't want you taking out your frustrations on me."

That caused her to burst into a deep throaty laugh, until she leaned back in her matching chair and said: "Gimme some sugar, Jack. I need a little taste," and we shared a lingering soulful kiss.

She finally broke off the kiss and leaned all the way back into the full-reclining position.

"Pretty dumb of him," I murmured, mostly to myself.

18

She spoke in a matching weary tone. "I guess he assumed I'd never have the balls to ever go back there."

I wanted to say it, but there seemed no reason. That word had once again reared its ugly head. To assume does nothing but make an ASS out of U and ME or . . . in this case, U first, and HIM last.

"What are you thinking, Jack?"

I pondered the question a moment, then said: "I doubt he'll ever assume anything again." I know I never will.

THE BULL

By Edgar Brown

One bright summer day I came to the breakfast table with my new fishing rod, which I leaned against the wall behind my chair. My mother watched me wolf down my breakfast and asked me why I was in such a hurry.

"I'm going fishing," I said. I didn't tell her I was going to ride my bike up Boulder Canyon. Ever since I got a bike on my seventh birthday, I had been riding all over Boulder, each time going a little farther from home. Now I wanted to ride up the canyon. I had often accompanied my parents when they drove through the canyon on the way to visit friends. To me, Boulder Canyon was an awesome place, surrounded by high mountains, rocks and rushing water. I wanted an adventure and going there promised to be just that.

Boulder lies among the foothills of the Rocky Mountains. Viewed from Denver in the east, the mountains look like an approaching tidal wave. The canyon winds its way west into the mountains beside Boulder Creek. The road hugs the canyon, with steep mountains on one side and high above Boulder Creek on the other. There is a dam at the top of the canyon, and high above it a glacier that supplies water to the City of Boulder.

The creek runs through a park near downtown. Fly fishermen are a common sight along its banks. Dressed in their waders and with creels slung over their shoulders, they whip their fly rods back and forth, arching their lines across the water to tempt trout with their lures. I often rode my bike to the park and followed anglers along the creek. I loved talking with them and seeing the fish in their creels.

A few anglers venture up the canyon where the creek is deep and swift, rushing over the rocks with a deafening roar. Because the footing is dangerous, these anglers often fish from the safety of bridges that cross the creek to the few tourist cabins on the other side.

I had good luck fishing with a bamboo pole and baiting my hook with worms. I persuaded my parents to buy me a new fishing rod—not a fly rod, but a bamboo pole that disassembled into two parts to make it easier to carry on my bike. I planned to take my fishing rod and hoped that anglers fishing in the canyon would invite me to join them on one of the bridges. My parents allowed me to cycle in the city, but I didn't think they would let me go into the canyon alone. I didn't risk asking for fear they would deny me permission. I was going fishing, and that was the truth.

After breakfast, I picked up my fishing rod and was about to leave when my mother reminded me that supper time was 6:00 o'clock. "I'll be home on time," I replied.

"Bring us some fish and be careful on your bike," my mother called out as I left to get my bike.

I tied my fishing pole to the bike, put the worms I'd gathered the day before in a small bag under my saddle and I rode off. I loved my bike like an Apache loved his pony—it freed me to explore the world.

I rode past my school on the way downtown and then turned west on the highway leading to the canyon. At the entrance, Flagstaff Mountain rose on the left. On the right is a hill topped by monolithic red rocks I had often climbed. This was the farthest west I'd ever ridden on my bike. From here I entered the canyon itself. As the canyon narrowed, the roar of the creek grew louder. I rode a short distance before reaching the first bridge. There were no anglers on the bridge, so I kept on riding, climbing higher and higher up the canyon.

The second bridge was also unoccupied. Finally, I reached a bridge where I found three anglers casting their lines. I got off my bike, walked onto the bridge and unloaded my fishing rod. One of the anglers welcomed me, saying he hoped I would bring them some luck.

"We've used all our flies, but so far none of us has caught a fish," said the friendly angler. They watched me put my rod together, bait my hook with a worm and toss my line into the water. Anglers generally look down their noses at people who use worms for bait, but they must have thought it was okay because I was a kid.

For the next hour and a half, I fished with the three men. They caught seven fish, but I didn't catch a single one. I was disappointed, but I'd had a good time fishing and sharing in the general excitement as each man reeled in a fish. Finally tiring of fishing, I tied my fishing pole to my bike, waved goodbye and started down the canyon. It was fun coasting instead of standing on the pedals like I had to on the climb up the canyon. I felt like I was flying, with the air whistling past my ears and my shirt flapping behind me like a flag. Going faster and faster, I leaned into the curves like a motorcyclist.

As I rounded the next curve, I suddenly had to stand on my brakes. Not twenty yards ahead a large bull with long horns was standing on the right side of the road. The bull didn't move, but he was eyeing me. I was afraid to ride past the bull. I couldn't go around him on the right because the mountain was too steep, and on the left, a dangerous drop to the creek. I turned around and rode back up the hill until I was far enough away from the bull to feel safe.

I thought about going back to the bridge to get help from the fishermen, but realized they had probably gone by now. Crossing the bridge where we fished wouldn't help because there was no road on the other side. The next bridge down the canyon led to a dirt road, but that bridge was below the bull. I began to think seriously about looking for a place farther up the canyon where I might be able to climb the mountain and make my way east to Boulder. I didn't like the idea because it was easy to get lost in the mountains, and I'd have to leave my bike behind. There was so little traffic in the canyon, it didn't occur to me to wait and get help from a passing motorist.

I walked along trying to decide what to do when I remembered seeing water pipes that crossed the creek somewhere farther up the canyon. I got on my bike and started riding. Sure enough, I found the water pipes a short distance ahead. Two oval shaped pipes some six inches apart crossed the creek about five feet above the water. To my delight, I saw a dirt road on the other side. I was sure it led to the bridge that crossed the creek below the bull.

I lifted my bike onto my right shoulder. Putting my left foot on the first pipe, I got on the other pipe and waited a moment to get my balance. I leaned to the left to offset the weight of my bike and began to take little steps forward. It was only after I cleared the bank and was over the water that I realized my danger—I still had more than half way to go and was already having difficulty holding the bike. The closeness of the raging water distracted me. I almost panicked. I took a few more steps and stopped; the bike was slipping off my shoulder. I managed to sit down on the pipes while holding the bike across my legs. I rested a few moments before attempting to stand again. I struggled to a standing position, and again began to move forward.

The roar of the creek was deafening, but I could hear someone yelling at me. I turned my head carefully to keep from losing my balance and saw a man wildly waving his arms and motioning me to come back. In my relief and excitement at being rescued, I turned around too quickly and my bike suddenly slipped off my shoulder. I grabbed the handlebar, and even though the bike was now hanging below the pipes, I refused to let go. With all my strength, I pulled the bike back up on the pipes and managed to get it on my shoulder. I forced myself to move faster while I still had enough strength left. This made it easier to keep my balance, and I finally reached the end of the pipes where the man was waiting.

"Are you trying to kill yourself?" yelled the man.

"I wanted to get away from the bull," I replied.

"What bull?"

"There's a bull beside the road down there, and I'm afraid to pass him on my bike."

"Let's put your bike in my car, and I'll drive you down the canyon," said the man.

Relieved, I helped the man put my bike in the trunk of his car. We started driving down the canyon. We rounded the curve where I thought I'd seen the bull, but the bull was gone.

"I might be mistaken about the exact place, but we should come to the bull very soon," I explained.

The man drove on without comment. We continued down the canyon. There was no sign of the bull. When we reached the mouth of the canyon, the man let me out of the car and unloaded my bike. "Stay off those pipes," he ordered and abruptly drove away. It was clear to me the man didn't believe there was a bull.

As I cycled home, I wondered whether or not I'd really seen the bull. But where could the bull have gone? He certainly didn't climb the mountain. The only other way the bull could have gone was across one of the bridges, yet the nearest bridge was so far down the canyon we would have passed him in the car.

When I got home, I didn't tell my parents what happened, even though I wanted to. They would have been angry because I'd gone into the canyon without permission. I kept thinking about the bull. Even though the bull seemed real to me, I was beginning to have doubts myself. I'd only seen the bull once and then for only a brief moment. Perhaps I imagined it after all.

The next morning my father was reading the paper. He suddenly looked up. "Listen to this," he said, lifting the paper. "Yesterday afternoon, police responding to a call for help from residents in western Boulder; found a large bull wandering through the neighborhood. It required several officers to round up the bull, which police later learned had escaped from a ranch south of Boulder."

CROSSING THE LINE

By Edgar Brown

In the summer of 1944, my friend Bob and I were asleep in our camp beside the Colorado River when what sounded like a stampede woke us up. The rumble was headed in our direction. We jumped up in time to see a bunch of armadillos rushing by. The almost unbelievable noise these creatures make running through the field belies their small size.

Now fully awake, Bob and I lit our kerosene lamp and sat around talking. We noticed lights across the river at the base of Mt. Bonnell, a mountain outside Austin, Texas. The mountain is very steep and the path leading down to the water difficult, if not dangerous. But fishermen make the effort because the large rock at the bottom makes a good platform from which to fish.

In fact, there are a number of places below Mt. Bonnell where one can fish at the water's edge and be sheltered by overhanging limestone shelves the river sculpted out of the mountain. But unlike the large rock where the fishermen were sitting, these spots can only be reached by boat.

The sound of the fishermen's laughter carried across the water. One laugh in particular caught our attention. It went on and on—"yah, yah, yah," endlessly renewing itself and, to us across the river, proved irresistibly infectious. We decided to ask if we could join the group. We packed our fishing rods in our boat—I say our boat, but the boat didn't really belong to us—we untied it from a landing in Taylor Slough and planned to return it on our way back. We paddled across the river to the rock where we found three Negroes fishing and another holding a rifle. They welcomed us and asked us to join them on the rock, which we did.

The oldest and shortest of the men said he was Reverend Brown, who stood up to introduce us to the others. I only remember the name of Leroy Eppright, probably because he was a huge man. Leroy saw me looking at the man with the rifle. I was a little nervous until he explained that they took turns standing watch with the rifle to kill water moccasins if they came towards the rock.

Bob and I tied up the boat and settled down on the rock with our fishing poles. We baited our lines with worms on hooks held to a shallow depth by brightly colored corks. Reverend Brown and the others baited two or three hooks with dough bait, which they formed into teardrop shaped chunks around the hooks. They tied the hooks to their lines with long leaders that allowed the hooks to spread out when heavy sinkers carried the bait to the bottom of the river.

We waited patiently watching our corks. If one disappeared, we quickly pulled up our rods. Our hosts, we noticed, sat staring at the ends of their rods. Upon the slightest movement of the tip of a rod, the man whose fishing rod it was yanked it up as hard as he could. To our utter surprise a large fish—a carp or a buffalo fish—would surface some twenty or thirty feet from the rock and swim back and forth trying to get away as the fisherman reeled in his line. More often than not, the fish weighed over five pounds and put up a good fight.

Suddenly, a water moccasin appeared in the arc of light the lamps behind us cast on the water. The rifleman stood up and fired twice killing the snake. I lost all interest in fishing and asked to be allowed to be the watchman for a while. The men agreed to let me do it, so I took over the rifle and stood watch, scanning the water as if my life depended on it. I recall being very excited and determined not to fail.

Nothing happened for a long time, but as fast as the first moccasin had appeared, another came into the circle of light heading straight for our rock. I stood up and aimed the rifle at the snake's head and waited for it to come closer. "Shoot it, shoot it," the men yelled and began to stand up ready to flee. I followed the snake's head as it came closer and closer to the rock—I didn't want to miss. I held my fire until the very last moment and shot at the tip of the snake's tail as it glided under our rock.

We all scrambled part way up the mountain. Leroy took the gun from me, but he didn't scold me. Without anyone saying a word, I knew that someone else would be taking my place. After waiting for about 15 minutes, the men decided it was safe to return to fish. Leroy went ahead with the rifle just in case. We were soon settled on the rock, fishing.

26

I felt somewhat subdued by all this, realizing that if I had been a Negro, the men would have expressed their anger at me in no uncertain terms and perhaps ordered Bob and me to leave. From the very beginning, I knew that in the segregated South, we had crossed the line. Socializing with Negroes was taboo. Worse, I understood that while Whites could waive the taboo, Negroes could not. Bob and I were violating the tenets of segregation and were in effect trespassing upon people who had no choice but to accept us.

Despite these misgivings, Bob and I enjoyed ourselves. We were intrigued with the way they fished. We caught nothing, but they caught a number of fish. They explained that the river near Mt. Bonnell was very deep, the kind of place where carp and buffalo fish grow large. To catch them required fishing at the bottom instead of dangling a line from a cork a few feet below the surface. We asked them where we could buy dough bait. At this, Reverend Brown laughed. He was the one whose laugh brought us to the rock in the first place. We joined in because of the laugh, not because we didn't know where to find dough bait.

Bob and I thought we might do better if we rowed over to one of the shelves a little farther up the river from the rock. Leroy agreed and wanted to go with us. The three of us got into the boat and paddled upstream about twenty-five yards where we found a good spot and settled down to fish.

Leroy got a bite and jumped up to give himself more room to land the fish. As he stood, however, his foot slipped on the rock and he fell into the river. He scrambled out and still managed to land a large catfish.

"Which one of those White boys fell in the river?" yelled Reverend Brown from the rock.

"It was Leroy," I shouted back.

"Yah, Yah, Yah," laughed Reverend Brown, louder and longer than ever.

We all joined in including, finally, Leroy himself.

When our new friends were preparing to leave, packing their gear for the trek up the mountain, Reverend Brown asked us whether we wanted to learn how to make dough bait. We replied that we did, and he gave us his address and invited us to come over the following Saturday. We thanked him and agreed to come. With that we said our goodbyes and paddled across the river to our camp.

When we returned to Austin after our camping trip, Bob and I made plans to visit Reverend Brown on Saturday. Neither of us had any hesitation about going to visit a Negro on the east side of Austin where Negroes lived. Some Whites also lived in east Austin and were free to do so. Negroes, on the other hand, couldn't live on the west side of Austin even if they wanted to, again demonstrating that segregation applied to Negroes, not to White people.

On Saturday, Bob and I took the bus to the east side of the city and walked from a bus stop to Reverend Brown's house. He greeted us at the door and invited us in. We met his wife who was friendly but seemed uncomfortable in our presence. Reverend Brown took us into the kitchen where he had already laid out everything needed to make dough bait.

As I recall, dough bait is largely white cornmeal. Reverend Brown poured hot water into a bowl, stirred in other ingredients and put the whole mess into a pan and fried it. The result looked like a large, thick pancake covered with a brown crust. After it cooled, he let us taste the crust, which proved to be quite edible. In fact, he said they often eat it while they're fishing. But the dough bait itself lay between the crusts—it was soft and malleable, ready to be squeezed around a hook. Reverend Brown kindly gave us the dough bait and hoped we would have better luck fishing. Before we left, he invited us to visit his church, and we agreed to come to the service the next day.

I can't recall how I felt about going to a Negro church—I do know that from the beginning of our friendship with Reverend Brown, Leroy and the others, Bob and I found ourselves in a world where we didn't belong and couldn't share with our White friends. Going to Reverend Brown's church was a way to show our new friends we didn't believe in segregation. To them, however, I'm sure our attendance would be just another example of exercising a choice they didn't have.

On Sunday, Bob and I went to the Negro church and sat in one of the front rows. Reverend Brown didn't introduce us or say anything to explain our presence. The service began with the choir and followed with readings from the Bible and the singing of hymns. Reverend Brown then gave his sermon. I became drowsy and fought to stay awake for fear of embarrassing our host, but in the end I fell asleep, just as I always did at church.

We stayed in touch with Reverend Brown and Leroy—we once got together with them at Leroy's house—but after the summer ended, I can't recall seeing them again. Bob and I went back to school and soon found ourselves caught up in the demands of our high school activities. We eventually lost touch with our new friends from the other side of town. If we reflected at all about segregation, we accepted it. After all, it wasn't our burden.

A DARK AREA

By Prayer Tisdale

My room glows of brightness

Slowly, my aching body gets up piece by piece

I see an image that smiles back at me

Then …that image has a river of tears

I see steam, and jump into that steam

I attempt on getting those streaming tears washed away

Images of the past flash

The pouring blood, the bully I faced daily

The bully would tell me, "Look at those scars, that face; she is the
most outrageous ugly monster."

That bully would take sharp objects and slice my precious brown skin

She would smile at me, and laugh a pure evil laugh

Finally an angel was sent from above

He fought a long rough battle with the devil, and killed it

My heart leaped of joy, and I twirled around him like a ballerina

I can't help but smile of joy, but cry that I was in a dark chamber

My angel tells me daily, "Forget about that chamber, you've escaped. You're in my arms now, and shall be safe."

I've shoved that bully from my mind, get off the steam, and celebrate the rest of my day. In fact, the rest of my life will be a celebration of joy.

EASY MONEY – HIGH RISKS

By J. J. Lenart

The five grave robbers had arrived in Quito, Ecuador, earlier that afternoon, and settled in the corner of a rundown *taberna* on the fringe of a slum. The air inside the tar paper shack was humid and smelled of stale tobacco and spilled beer. A pay phone mounted on the wall by their table was the only visible modern convenience in their makeshift office. All drank bottled beer, not concerned if any spilled onto the earthen floor.

These weren't run-of-the-mill looters who preyed on surface plots for gold teeth and rings. Their specialty was the theft of historical artifacts from archeological digs. The range of their enterprise was from Mexico to Chile.

The employer was a man named Jean-Claude Forquois, a heavyweight with the Pan American Cartel. The Frenchman's contribution to the vast illegal enterprise was the location and acquisition of gold, silver, gemstones, and priceless antiquities. He was known to be ruthless and had no qualms about enlisting the help of government officials for his material export.

A shrill ring of the phone prompted the shortest and leanest of the five to grab the handset from the cradle. "Hello?" He listened a few seconds and then said: "I understand. Tonight only."

The way the jobs worked was that Joaquín, the team's leader, was given a packet of detailed instructions for them to study. It included photos and photocopies of whatever drawings and architectural sketches existed. The only piece of the puzzle missing was the exact location of where to dig. Joaquín never received that piece of critical information until hours before the theft. This was a precaution by his employer to prevent a double-cross, of thieves stealing from thieves.

"We go now. It's an Inca burial site outside the small town of Papallacta, about fifty miles east of here. It's under the basement of a relic church from the days of the *conquistadores*. It's named Iglesia de Pesadumbre."

At a little past seven that evening, after they'd bought food and drink for the night ahead, Joaquín and his team left for Papallacta. Their transportation was a sixteen-year-old windowless van dented and marked with patches of rust and blotches of unmatched spray paint. It gave the appearance of a junk-yard refugee, and would not be obvious or out of place.

As they drove, the leader reviewed their plan. "Remember, *compadres*, this is a one-shot deal. Señor Forquois says we have to finish our business tonight."

"Why the rush?" the man riding shotgun asked. He was Joaquín's younger brother, Juan. "Why don't we do what we usually do? Bottle up the place so we can take our time. How much trouble can a few old priests be?"

"The rush is because *el jefe* says so," Joaquín answered as he turned onto a freshly-paved highway and better driving. "Also, because he's moving his operation to Panama for a while. One of his highly-placed government sources told him to get out of South America for his health."

"Why?"

"He didn't say. Probably because things are getting too hot down here. You know he's got another court appearance in Bogotá this week? Anyway, like I said before, this is supposed to be a light load. Jewelry and gemstones, for the most part. It shouldn't take much time." Joaquín knew that if the find had turned up anything heavy, there would have been more people involved, with more time allowed. By heavy, that meant large amounts of gold and silver, or even carved stone. "There might be a few pieces of gold and silver," he added, "but, for sure, there's supposed to be a fortune in gems."

"How did Señor Jean-Claude learn of this?" Juan persisted.

Joaquín answered in a monotone, watching traffic for any police cars: "Some archeologist — a local Indian I think — discovered it a few days ago."

"What about the guards you mentioned?" a gravelly voice asked from the back seat.

"Four guards, is what I was told. Shouldn't be a big problem. Probably peasants hired by the church or the Ecuadorian Ministry to keep snoopers out. Either way, you know they aren't being paid much," and Joaquín chuckled out loud.

On arriving at Papallacta, it was already nighttime. They found the church about a mile outside of town, situated with its back against a large piece of granite outcropping. They parked the van behind a turn in the road, and approached on foot.

Joaquín, like the others, was small-framed and wiry, but deceptively strong. He was short at 5'2", and maybe weighed 120 pounds. With the dark olive fatigues he and his team wore, they were nearly invisible in the darkness. Now, he was wet with perspiration from the anticipation and excitement of his work.

As they got closer, Juan asked his brother in a whisper, "You smell what I smell? That's campfire smoke. Someone's cooking."

"Shhh!"

They snooped around the area and found that there were actually five guards, one more than the caller had alerted them about. They had the look of peasant farmers, and only one was watching at the old church's basement door. The others were stationed at random perimeter locations, where there was a place to sit and sleep.

There was a problem, though. The area around the church was supposed to be deserted, but it now appeared that the grounds had been occupied by several families. Smoldering campfires showed dim light at a half-dozen locations, and a low cloud of smoke blanketed the area. Several old men and women shuffled from hut to hut, occasionally stopping by a fire for heat or to talk.

"What is this?" Juan whispered close by Joaquín's ear. He sounded agitated. "This place was supposed to be deserted!"

"How the hell am I supposed to know?" came the curt answer. "They appear to be Indians and, by their clothes, they look like they belong in the sierra. Let's just take care of business."

From the light of the scattered campfires, Joaquín counted at least eight crude stone-and-wood dwellings that had already been completed. Another cluster was under construction. These people were not supposed to be here, he thought, and silently hoped that they would not be a problem or interfere.

* * *

By 10:30, the robbers had killed and hidden the bodies of the four perimeter guards. A sharp stiletto blade was Joaquín's preferred weapon for this kind of work. He simply placed the tip behind the ear and thrust it into the cranium. It was very effective, and precluded the need for a wrestling match with the victim or a lot of blood. The last guard, who had been found asleep by the basement door, had simply been flipped backward off his chair. His head hit the church's stone foundation with such force that his skull split open like a ripe melon.

Now that the team was at the sought-after entrance, they huddled in the dark shadow of a nearby shed. They were out of breath from running in the high-altitude air from one place of concealment to another, and also from having to deal with the bodies. So, they took a short rest and quickly reviewed their plan.

As soon as they opened the basement door, the quintet of thieves uncovered their first formidable obstacle. The stairway to the church's underground was filled with rubble — maybe a ton or more of loosely-packed dirt and stone. Their only access had been closed off.

The five looked around, as if expecting someone to emerge from the dark and laugh at them as the fools of a joke. No one appeared. All they could see nearby was a small mound of filthy and tattered woven baskets that, obviously, had been used to refill the opening.

Joaquín was beside himself. Señor Forquois did not tolerate failure very well. The team had to get to the underground site, and he and his four *huaqueros* would never be able to move so much dirt and rock by themselves. This was not going to be easy. So, Joaquín sent two of the diggers back to the battered van to fetch other weapons. They needed to enlist some help.

Joaquín and his comrades woke the entire village of peasants and forced them into the church's empty vestibule. There were nearly sixty of them, a mix of very young and very old. Men and women, boys and girls, in nearly equal numbers. The thieves used the threat of their weapons to quiet the assembled crowd; and Joaquín ordered his brother, Juan, and another digger to move the five dead guards inside with the terrified villagers to emphasize the robbers' resolve. A few women and children sobbed over the dead men.

Joaquín wondered silently where the young adults could be, especially the mothers of so many children. He was further frustrated when he realized that these people did not speak Spanish. All they spoke was some ancient Andean dialect that he couldn't understand.

35

Quechua, he thought he heard one of the peasants say. For that reason, it took nearly another half-hour to explain what he wanted. To do this, he drew sketches in the dirt by the basement door.

Over the next three hours, shifts of weary peasant men and women removed most of the dirt and debris that concealed the entrance to the dig site. The most difficult part was clearing the steep stairway, as that had to be completely dug out. Joaquín was relieved to find that the entire labyrinth of basement tunnels beneath the church had not been filled in. As soon as the digging was completed, the exhausted peasants were herded back inside the church. Four had died in the night from exhaustion or stroke, or whatever, and several others shuffled along with difficulty. Two of the diggers, Miguel and a fourteen year old they called Chico, stayed outside to keep the hostages quiet and guard the church door.

Joaquín, Juan, and another of the team finally began, and descended the freshly excavated stone stairway. They proceeded slowly, with scarred and dirty miners' hats strapped on their heads. The head-gear also supported a high-intensity light. Battery packs tied around their waists provided the energy to illuminate their way. Each man also had a rheostat to control the brightness. Too much light in the confined spaces below could be blinding. Their tools were in back-packs; and finely woven nylon mesh loot-bags were also stuffed in their packs.

The Iglesia de Pesadumbre was an old building, first constructed in the early 17th century. The basement passages were low and narrow, with walls constructed of thick stone. In fact, the church was built on an ancient Inca foundation. That was a common practice of the Spanish conquerors of olden days. But the low ceilings meant that everyone had to walk with a bent-over stoop. The main passage, according to the sketch that Joaquín carried, bisected the church's foundation. There were six lateral passages off the main corridor, but only one interested Joaquín.

Even though the church had been reconstructed three or four times over the past four hundred years, the sub-surface areas hadn't been altered. As the men passed and looked inside small empty chambers, they found the rotted remnants of heavy doors that had once closed off the tiny rock walled rooms. Store rooms, probably. Almost two dozen of them. All empty.

As was their past practice, the last man in the column carried a spool of light-blue monofilament fishing line. That was Luis's job. He was called the lineman. As they walked, the lineman allowed the thin nylon line to be fed out. If he ran out, he carried another thousand-yard spool in his pack. This was an old habit that had served them well, in case they lost their way or their lighting. Once, while searching for a Mayan tomb in Guatemala, a digger had dropped and lost their map in a deep hole. The line had been their only hope of escaping the maze of tunnels on that trip.

At the dead end of the long trunk passage was a T-intersection.

"Okay," said Joaquín. "We're at the end. Now, we backtrack to the first lateral passage on our right. Got it?"

"Hold on a second," said Luis. "I need to reel in the line as we go."

"Go ahead. You're the first to go back, anyway," directed the leader.

The party of three treasure hunters took the next few minutes to retrace their steps and get to the correct tunnel. Once there, they sat on the chilled stone floor and took a short break. The air was close and musty. Passing a canteen around, they shared a fruit juice drink that was loaded with sugar and caffeine additive. Then they started again.

Their destination was a small stone-walled room at the end of the lateral passageway. At the entry, each aimed their helmet-mounted lights into the room and trained the beams on the floor. Each entered cautiously, in turn, and looked around. They were wary of hidden traps, as they had encountered them before in such places.

Looking around the room, Juan said: "Hey, Joaquín. There's no hole here." He even went over to a large flat rock in a corner, and carefully slid it aside. Nothing underneath.

Joaquín fished in his pocket and retrieved the sketch of the room.

Before their leader could get his bearings with the rough drawing, Luis saw something dark in a corner. He trained his light to the spot, and spoke excitedly. "Joaquín! Juan! Look over here!"

The carved-out hole was obscured by a protruding piece of granite. And, to confound any intruders, the excavated opening was in an odd place — in a corner by the ceiling.

"Jesus, Mary, and Joseph!" exclaimed Juan. "Who in the name of Christ found this?"

"Like I said before. Some archeologist — according to the

37

packet," Joaquín answered. "An Indian. Works for the Ministry of History and Antiquities."

"Can we get into that hole?" Juan asked his second question.

"Shouldn't be a problem. Anyway, according to the information we were given, that hole opens up to a larger chamber below."

"Yeah, but first we have to get past that small opening. Christ, man, the entry's so flat. How the hell are we going to get up there to get in?"

"Stop complaining," Joaquín chided his brother. "Just help me get up there to take a look." The opening had been made by removing one medium-sized chiseled boulder. It was the one that Juan had moved to look for a hole in the floor, and it was at least fifteen inches deep.

Juan got on his hands and knees by the wall, and Joaquín stood on his back. In that way, Joaquín could carefully lean into the hole and look around. He spent almost a minute with his inspection, and then lowered a rope with a flashlight tied to the end into the black pit. When he pushed himself out of the hole, he sat on the dusty stone floor with Juan and Luis and reported.

"No problem that I could see. There's a vertical shaft that drops about twenty feet. There's an open chamber below that, and it looks to be another ten or twelve feet deep."

"So, we're looking at a 30-foot drop?" asked the brother.

"Right. We can move that rock over here and anchor our rope. It must be at least 200 pounds. As long as we go one at a time, there shouldn't be any trouble."

A thick braided nylon rope was already knotted with climbing holds. Fifty-feet of the 100-foot rope was dropped into the dark hole. The end was tied around the large stone, after it had been moved from the corner to a spot beneath the hole.

Joaquín went first. Mostly because he enjoyed being the first to discover a new find. But, then again, no one ever argued about being first in. Joaquín could have the thrill, everyone on the team had agreed years ago. No one ever knew what was in the holes they ventured into.

With Juan and Luis's help, Joaquín was helped to stand on his hands with his back facing the wall. The two men picked him up over their heads to the ceiling, and guided his feet and legs into the narrow opening. Once he could bend his legs at the knees, he was pushed

38

further in so that his lower back rested on the rock sill of the hole. In that position, Joaquín slowly turned onto his stomach. It was tight, as the hole was so flat; but he made it. From that position, it was an easy transition into the vertical shaft. Using the knotted climbing rope, he descended to the chamber floor thirty feet below.

For five minutes, Juan and Luis waited patiently to hear from their leader. Both stood with an ear near the opening, and kept quiet in case Joaquín called out from the vertical shaft. They were shaken from their vigil when the climbing rope became taught again. Shortly, Joaquín's head and upper torso appeared in the hole. He was filthy and filled the opening. His breathing was labored from the climb, and he was perspiring profusely. He also wore a wide smile on his face.

"Well, what did you find?" rushed Juan.

"A king's treasure, that's what. Take off my hat, and be careful."

Juan undid the strap that held the miner's hard hat on Joaquín's head, and once it was off, carefully extracted a glistening yellow necklace. Luis looked over his shoulder, and gasped. The piece must have been beaten from solid gold, and felt like it could have weighed two or three pounds. But it wasn't the gold that captured Juan's attention. It was the size of the inlaid emerald stone in the center of the medallion. "Mother of Christ!" exclaimed Juan.

"Amazing, isn't it? That one was around the largest of the mummies I found. Must have been a queen, or something. And, that's not all."

"What do you mean?" Juan quizzed his sibling partner with a grin forming on his face.

"Whoever set this up really blew it. There's a couple of other mummified bodies down there, and jars of stones. Just like the packet described. But, there's a false wall down there, too. I can't believe anyone could have missed it. Especially an archeologist."

"What did you find there?"

"Gold and silver. A mountain of it. We'll never get it all out in one night."

"So, how do you want to do this?"

"We'll get the stuff we were sent for. Then, we'll see if there's time for anything else. Christ, man, the gems and jewelry are going to be a load by themselves."

"Do you want me down there?"

"No. No need. You're too thick around the middle for this hole, anyway. Send down the kid, Chico. He's the skinniest of the other two. You stay up here with Luis, and move the stuff we send up."

"Got it," agreed Juan.

"Let's get started, then. Set that necklace aside. I'm going to try and keep it for myself. Pick out something for yourself and the others when I send the goods up. There's plenty for a souvenir for everyone."

With nothing more to add, Joaquín pushed himself back into the vertical void and the treasure below. Juan sent Luis back for Chico who was standing guard. Luis also took the first of their loot with him: the gold necklace with the large emerald.

When Luis returned with Chico, Juan explained the layout of the site. With the instructions passed on, the slender youth was hoisted to squirm into the hole by the ceiling and shortly disappeared.

Juan unpacked a 100-foot coil of narrow nylon rope. This was for retrieving the treasure. He lowered the smaller rope's end with the rolled up loot-bags tied on.

Within a few minutes, there was a tug on the treasure line. It was the signal to begin pulling. The load felt heavy, but not impossible to haul. The problem came when the loot-bag couldn't fit through the hole. Juan called past the plugged-up opening, and into the vertical pit. Joaquín would have to help.

Joaquín sent Chico up the knotted climbing rope to free the bag. The youth encountered some difficulty, though, in handling the bag full of stones and jewelry. It was wedged tight in the narrow opening. He tried to force it through the hole while still holding onto his climbing rope, but he couldn't budge it. As the digger had a very slight physique to allow him access into these tight places, he lacked the bulky strength to force the sack through the hole. So, to help with his leverage, he reached upward past the full bag to see if he could find something to hold onto.

He was fortunate. There was something. "Hold on a moment, Juan," the young digger spoke in a strained muffled voice.

"No problem, man. You're the one holding on," and Juan chuckled at the youth's predicament. He could hear the digger struggling on the other side of the full loot-bag wedged into the wall hole.

"I only need a little more leverage. And this hand-hold here should do . . ."

Juan hadn't been listening with much attention. After all, the problem was only to force the bag through the hole. But, as soon as he understood what his young partner had said, he panicked. "Don't touch . . ." was all that Juan got out of his mouth.

As soon as the rumble started, there was a muffled yell. But, Chico's pleading call didn't last long.

With the first sound of the collapsing shaft, Juan jumped off the stone he had been standing on. His backward motion away from the hole had him slam into Luis, who was directly behind him. They both stumbled backward into the small room's wall, and collapsed to the floor.

Everything happened so fast.

Even though they hadn't done much but collide and fall, they were both dazed and breathing heavily. Fortunately, they had their miners' hats on to protect their heads as they smacked the nearby wall.

"What's wrong?" gasped Luis, not fully understanding the nature of the problem.

The initial earth-shaking noise from the hole in the wall stopped momentarily. Juan untangled himself from Luis, and rushed back to the hole. The bag was gone, as was the digger trying to dislodge it. A cloud of fine dust began to seep into the room from the black void.

"Joaquín! Joaquín!" Juan shouted to his brother. "Chico!" There was no sound from either of them. It was eerily quiet, except for the excited breathing of the two men in the small cramped space.

More fine dust escaped from the hole and formed a wispy cloud in the tiny room. Then came an ominous creaking sound. Faint at first — then growing louder.

Juan pushed himself back off the stone. He was frantic, now. "We have to get out of here!" he shouted, and pushed himself past Luis who was still on the floor.

Juan scurried as fast as he could move, following the nylon line. He yelled back over his shoulder as he moved: "Come on, Luis! Move! This whole place is falling in!"

As he rushed, he bounced from side-to-side off the walls of the narrow underground passageway. The air was stale, but wasn't dusty. Not yet, anyway. He could feel... then hear... the sounds of the earth moving beneath him ... and the tearing of old timber and snapping of

41

smaller pieces of dry wood. The church was breaking up. Dust and dry dirt started to fall into the passageway from the old support beams above. He kept running. The thin nylon line slipped past his cupped palm as he went. Sharp pains began to shoot from his knees and into his thighs from the odd posture of his race. He fell, and crawled on hands and knees for several feet. It seemed to help relieve the sharp stabs in his cramped legs.

He got back up and continued his labored awkward run.

Juan ran in that duck-walk crouch all the way back to the landing of the stone stairs, and collapsed with exhaustion. He waited there, covered in filth, trying to catch his breath. He was shortly joined by the lineman, Luis, stumbling and gasping for air. They were both breathing hard. Forcing their lungs to work.

"What's going on?" Luis expelled a question between breaths.

"I don't know," Juan rushed his answer. "Let's just get the hell out of here!" and he pushed himself back to his feet. He grabbed Luis by his shirt, and yelled this time, "Come on!"

"What about Joaquín and Chico?"

"What 'Joaquín'?" Juan answered. There is no more Joaquín. He's gone. They're both gone." Suddenly, more dust and dirt started to fall on them from above. "Come on!" Juan insisted as he dragged Luis up the stone stairs. The church had already started to move above them.

Both men emerged from the basement and ran to the church's front door. They found their lone guard, Miguel, and all the captive villagers gone. Thinking Miguel had moved back to the van and that the peasants had fled, they turned and ran. After a few hundred feet, they heard the church behind them breaking up and falling in on itself.

Juan and Luis stopped and turned to watch the shaking shadow of the crumbling church in the dim dawn light. Both breathed heavily.

Eventually, Luis asked between his pants for air, "What happened back there?"

"I really don't know. One moment Chico was feeling around for some kind of leverage, then he was gone. Shit! he must have grabbed some kind of lever in the shaft. Stupid idiot!" Juan exclaimed, and spit into the early morning light. It was a slurry of saliva and dust. Then he added: "It was probably a hidden trap left there by the builders of the foundation."

"You mean like Incas?" Luis asked, sounding incredulous.

42

"Incas. Moche. Makes no difference who," Juan answered. "All those bastards used to leave traps everywhere. They didn't care who they killed."

Both men were suddenly startled by the coughing sound of their van's engine as it started. Before they could turn and continue their escape, Juan and Luis were ambushed from behind.

FIRST SOLO

By F. Clifton Berry, Jr.

Rex Taylor, Certified Flight Instructor (CFI), occupied the right seat of the Cessna 172. I, the student pilot, occupied the left seat. The airplane, with tail number 73171, belonged to the Andrews Air Force Base flying club. After departing Andrews at 9:00 a.m. local time we were flying at 3,500 feet altitude on a heading of 110 degrees, bound for the airport at Easton, Maryland, across the Chesapeake Bay.

This was another instruction flight in my quest to achieve a private pilot certificate. The flight took place on Saturday, April 18, 1981. Rex and I had flown as instructor and student in the past few weeks. We complied with all the Federal Aviation Administration (FAA) requirements on the ground and in the air, academic and actual combined. With Rex and other instructors I had logged 21.8 hours of dual flight instruction, passing the FAA minimum of twenty hours.

Today might be the day of my first solo flight. Rex and another instructor had told me to be ready, just in case. "Better to be prepared than surprised" was one of the sayings they often quoted. In the hour before takeoff we performed the preparation. I planned the route to Easton. I memorized the airfield's critical data, such as runway lengths and headings, radio frequencies, and more. To prevent surprise (or faulty memory), I wrote all those bits of essential information onto the paper mounted on the pilot's kneeboard strapped atop my right leg.

Now we are across Chesapeake Bay, with Newnam/Easton Field in sight. We have selected its Runway 22 for landing. We descend to 2,500 feet and fly over the field. The runway is clear and no aircraft are moving on the ramps. The wind sock is rising about halfway, indicating a wind of about ten knots. The wind direction is from the south, almost exactly 180 degrees.

Over the radio, I announce our intention to land, just in case some other aircraft are nearby. I reduce power and descend to the pattern altitude of 1,100 feet. Rex suggests that we make a straight-in

44

approach, so I keep us on a heading of 220 degrees right toward Runway 22. I perform the "Before Landing" checklist, reduce power, and aim for a spot about 300 feet down the runway. The landing is okay, and we roll to a stop. Rex points toward the ramp area. I taxi 73171 over there and come to a stop.

Rex tells me to keep the engine running. He doffs his headset, unbuckles his seat belt and shoulder harness, and swings his door open. He says, "OK, Clif, it's time for your first solo.
Take her up, stay within the pattern, and perform three takeoffs and landings. Then come back to pick me up."

"Wilco, Rex," I yell out in glee. "Wilco!" Rex dismounts and shuts the door. He stands erect, offers a snappy salute (we're both former Army officers), and waves toward the end of the runway. I return the salute and concentrate on the immediate tasks.

Rex mentioned three takeoffs and landings. It's another reminder of the saying that other pilots have mentioned: "Keep the number of your landings equal to the number of your takeoffs."

Now it's time for serious concentration. I perform the "Before Takeoff" checklist of fifteen actions, then taxi to the end of Runway 22. I press the radio switch and transmit information to other aircraft in the neighborhood. "Easton traffic, Cessna 73171. Taking off on Runway Two-two. Remaining in pattern." I enter the runway and make sure that 73171's nose wheel rests on the center line. With both toes pressing on the brake pedals I advance the throttle to its maximum. The engine is running smoothly. A quick survey of the instrument panel shows all the gadgets in the proper position. I release the brakes and 73171 accelerates down the runway. Glancing at the empty right-hand seat proves that I am here all alone . . . solo.

What next? "Next" is time to check airspeed. It reaches fifty-five knots and I apply back pressure to the control wheel. 73171 leaves the ground and accelerates. When it reaches seventy knots I pull the control wheel back a bit more. I lower the left wing slightly to compensate for the modest crosswind. We climb smoothly to 1,100 feet. That is pattern altitude, so I level off and turn left 90 degrees and begin to enjoy the flying. Flying solo!

Another of Rex's aviation sayings pops into my mind. "Flying is the second-greatest thrill known to man. Landing is the first."

My first solo takeoff is complete. The first solo landing is near. I scan the vicinity widely as possible, all-around and up and down. The right-hand seat remains empty. But then I realize that the Great Chief Flight Instructor up in the sky is with me. I thank Him for His presence. I turn left again and we fly the downwind leg on a heading of 040 degrees parallel to Runway 22.

Before every maneuver I broadcast my intentions over the radio. We turn left onto the base leg and left again to begin the final approach. I perform all steps of the "Before Landing" checklist. We are lined up with Runway 22's center line again, reducing power and lowering the wing flaps to ease the airspeed down to fifty-five knots. The aiming point is just past the "22" numbers painted on the end of the runway. I ease the throttle back to the "idle" position.

The "22" numbers grow ever-larger and pass beneath us. I lift the nose a bit. *My gosh, it's quiet in here.* Touchdown! The main wheels touch the runway and stay there. No bounce, thank you. I lower the nose wheel and apply the brakes gently. We leave the runway and enter the taxiway to return to the takeoff end of the runway, performing the "After Landing" checklist.

Two more takeoffs and landings remain. I take my time, use the checklists, and go easy on the controls and switches. All goes smoothly. I thank the Great Chief Flight Instructor after each landing.

Rex raises a "thumbs-up" as we stop for him to climb into 73171. He shakes my hand. "Congratulations, Clif! You've completed your first solo. Let's do one more takeoff and landing here, and then head back to Andrews." We do it, and are soon back at Andrews, performing the post-flight check on 73171 at the flying club's hangar.

My confidence level is a bit higher than before we took off from Andrews earlier in the morning. Then I recall another saying. This one is from an Air Force general who reinforced my quest to become a pilot. "Just remember this: you are always a student in an airplane. You learn from every flight." He is right.

Rex endorses my logbook with the language that the FAA requires. Other members of the flying club are smiling. One hands Rex a pair of scissors. An American flying tradition is about to happen. "OK, Clif, pull out your shirttail and turn around." I comply with the order and feel the tugs as Rex snips off a large piece of fabric. He clips it to an over-size set of pilot wings formed from foil wrap, and hands it to me with congratulations. Other club members join in. My first solo has happened. What a feeling!

46

The first solo flight is a milestone for every aspiring pilot. It is also a motivator; an incentive for continuing the rigorous trek to achieving the private pilot license.

Seven months and forty-eight flying hours later I passed the written and flight tests, and qualified as a Private Pilot, Single-Engine Land. The shirttail hangs in my office, a happy and enduring reminder.

That April 18 morning remains unforgettable. I have another reason to consider the date even more cherished. On April 18, 1958 I asked Irene, "Will you marry me?" She said, "Yes," unforgettably linking us forever.

A FOLK HERO OF SORTS

By Patricia Boswell Kallman

My daughter has been studying tall tales and folk heroes in her AP Lit class. Her assignment is to write an essay creating a folk hero for her school. She's been staring at her laptop and complaining for quite some time now, so I challenge her to a write-off. We will each come up with a folk hero for our respective high schools and see who can write the better story. I suffer a few unkind remarks about me not being able to remember back that far. In my best, supportive-parent tone of voice, I mutter something about "wet behind the ears," and we settle in at our computers.

I sit and stare at the screen a while contemplating a worthy subject. There are a few contenders. There's the biology teacher who once allowed us to have a whipped cream battle as long as we cleaned up afterwards. Because we stuck to everything for weeks, we had to keep cleaning every day. That was my last whipped cream battle. Then there's our chemistry teacher. Each day, we left our belongings in his classroom, went to lunch and then returned to his room for class. Although he threatened, he never did send any of us to the principal's office, even though we daily rearranged his molecular models. They were just too much like Tinker Toys to resist. We made it up to him though. We threw a party for him one day when he came back from lunch. We had roasted marshmallows over the Bunsen burners and served cider in beakers. Those two teachers made bio and chem tolerable for me.

There is, however, one stand-out candidate. Mr. Mortimer was affectionately known as Mr. Mo, and our class lucked out when we elected him our advisor. He stayed with us through our four years of high school. He was a math teacher and a rabble-rouser, smart and witty with the personality of a con man. He laughed at us, himself and the world in general. He was, dare I say it, yes, irreverent. I had Mr. Mo for algebra, geometry and finally, trig. He ultimately agreed with me that I would probably be happier in German III than taking calculus from him.

Mr. Mo called us the "curriculum guinea pigs" and "lab rats." In our school system, we were the first accelerated section to go through both the junior and senior high schools as a unit. "It's easy, ladies and gentlemen. It's just a *trick*, and I'm going to teach *you* the trick." An axiom would become a trick, and we knew the secret! It was slight-of-mind for twenty-two fledgling math magicians. He conned us with cosines, and we raced to solve any problem he put on the blackboard.

His style was offhand. "Miss Boswell, I shot off my mouth and told the big cheese you and your pals here could write a junior class variety show for us to put on. It could pay for a pretty ritzy prom." So, we wrote it, and it made a gargantuan amount of money! Our junior-senior prom was spectacular.

I have it on good authority, since my cousin is married to the high school French teacher, that Mr. Mo stood up for me, figuratively and literally, once during a faculty meeting. Our principal did not like teenagers. Don't ask me why he chose to be a high school principal. He announced to the faculty that I set a bad example for other students because I had too many extracurricular activities. "She's in band, glee club, editor of the newspaper, works on the yearbook, is treasurer of Tri Hi Y, and in the photography club."

Mr. Mo exploded to his feet and yelled, "For cryin' out loud, Fred, you forgot she wrote the class play this year! She's also in National Honor Society, so she must get good grades. We should have a whole friggin' school full of these bad examples!" So, our white knight slayed a dragon for me that day. It wasn't only me. Almost every kid in the class had a nice story about Mr. Mo helping them or going to bat for them.

At graduation, in front of the whole school and our parents, we embarrassed him as we presented him with a color TV, an easy chair, a cashmere sweater and slippers. Later, on the sly, in the school parking lot, surrounded by two hundred cheering graduates, a case of scotch made its way from one car trunk to another.

At our twenty-fifth year reunion after a couple of beers, I thanked him for standing up for me that time in the faculty meeting. The boyish grin flashed beneath the graying hair. "Oh hell, Pat, it was too good to pass up! He left himself wide open. Believe me, I really did it more for me than you!" No altruism in this man. Like all good folk heroes, he just did what needed to be done.

My daughter's folk hero is a custodian who cleans up more than just the hallways of the school. She leaves notes on whiteboards for teachers explaining how to coax the best work from their students, and slips of paper in student lockers, advising how to get through the pangs of first love. She grows good grades and diplomas in a basement garden, and maintains the invisible wall around the school that keeps out undesirable substances and weapons. I may have lost this writing contest, but I do still know a *trick* or two that I can interpolate into real life!

FOR EVERYTHING THERE IS A SEASON

By Molly Templar

Red, yellow and orange colored leaves drifting to the earth…

A whirlwind of leaves on a blustery day…

The last song of the sparrow preparing to migrate south…

Sun low in the sky giving way to the full, orange harvest moon…

The scent of crisp air mixed with the earthy aroma of hickory, elm, and oak….

Crunch of leaves and acorns underfoot…

A bright orange pumpkin in the field…

     Unforgettable signs of autumn.

Fluffy white snowflakes blanketing evergreens…

Unique snowflakes gently falling to earth…

Contrast of a bright red cardinal perched on a snowy white limb…

The fresh scent of pristine white snow…

The clean taste of snowflakes landing on my tongue…

Silence of snow piling into soft drifts…

The joy of snowmen and snowballs…

     Unforgettable signs of winter.

Purple and yellow crocus pushing up through the last spring snow...

Bright red and yellow cup-shaped tulips with elegant long stems...

The whiff of fertile garden mulch blanketing new flowerbeds...

The rich caroling of the red robin...

Fuzzy caterpillars inching through blades of green grass...

Rain gently pattering against the windowsill...

The smell of fresh cut grass...

      Unforgettable signs of spring.

Sunshine's warmth seeping into every bone..

Feeling ocean spray on your face...

Grains of sand trickling between your toes...

Fragrance of onions, peppers, and tomatoes in the garden...

Gentle breeze at sunset on the lake...

Butterflies flitting among vibrant, multicolored wildflowers...

Baby robins leaving the nest...

      Unforgettable signs of summer.

Each season is distinctive and...

Like the cycles of life, leaves...

      Unforgettable, enduring memories.

GAMBLING

By Richard Katchmark

Unforgettable is a big word for me. At age sixty-eight I am adept at recalling so many memories that I classify as unforgettable. It is last week that seems a little foggy right now. Those older remembrances comprise a large number dealing with my wife (Carol), our children, grandchildren, The Creator of the Universe, relatives, friends, strangers, and employment. I know I must share with you only one specific event in this anthology. My mind now races to an incident while I was on a business trip to Philadelphia.

I spent two days and one overnight on business. I promised my wife that I would only *blow* one hundred dollars on gambling if I decided to visit the Atlantic City casinos. On the first day I finished my business activity and business dinner at around seven o'clock. Decision time: Back to my hotel room or drive to Atlantic City; Atlantic City won.

I lost a quick fifty dollars at the blackjack table then walked away. I hoped I would recoup my fifty bucks at the slot machines. I chose the one-dollar machines to get the money back quickly. Two machines where I deposited silver dollars sucked up my second fifty—fast. I was in Atlantic City for less than an hour and was down one hundred dollars. I remembered my promise to Carol and decided to return to the hotel. To recover from being angry with the Casino for taking my money so quickly, I decided to have one cold beer before my drive back to Philadelphia.

I took a seat at a table in the bar because my favorite seats, the barstools, were all occupied. I sat and began thinking of Carol; I wished she were here with me. Then a scantily dressed waitress came by and took my order for one draft beer. When she returned with the beer, she asked, "What are you thinking about? You seem so deep in thought sitting alone."

"My thoughts are of my wife and how I dislike traveling on business and being away from her."

I noticed her staring at me and then she asked, "Would you buy me a drink so I can sit with you and ask a few questions." Then she whispered, "I'm actually a prostitute working here but I'm not allowed to sit with any customer unless they buy me a watered-down drink."

She must have read the shocked look on my face and then she continued, "It's OK, my questions are not about prostitution. I just need a few minutes."

For some dumb-ass reason I agreed. She returned with a drink and sat down. "I'm Karen; I think all men are pieces of shit. You are the first man I ever met who said he was thinking about his wife and how he missed her. I knew I needed to know why you felt like that."

"My wife is my best friend and she is the one I want to share all my life with, even though earning a living on business trips seems to interfere with our relationship."

Karen interrupted, "Would you listen to my story?"

"I would be glad to listen to you."

"It began when I was fourteen and my father walked in on me while I was showering and introduced me to sex. My mother had died one year earlier and at first I thought his subsequent visits to my bed were what a daughter should do. After my seventeenth birthday, I told him I didn't want to do that anymore. He forced himself on me one afternoon and I screamed and began to hate him. He stopped for a while and then I saw him in bed with my fourteen-year-old sister. I packed some clothes, took all the money from dad's wallet and ran away. I am a terrible person. I abandoned my sister to him. I hung out and stayed with two older boys who drove me to Atlantic City where they knew I could use my body to earn us money. They also enjoyed my body and introduced me to drugs. After a few years everything turned to shit and I ended up in jail. After serving my jail time, I came to this casino and was hired to serve drinks. I met Samantha who operates as a prostitute here and she showed how I could make real money as a prostitute while working at the casino. I stayed off the drugs and dumped my two boyfriends. Samantha found me an apartment. She helped me a lot, and now my life is the best it has ever been. I don't know what happened to my sister." She became silent and tears began rolling down her cheeks and she made no effort to stop them. I had no words to say.

From under her breath I heard, "Thank you for listening" and after a brief pause, she stated, "I resent all men, including my clients. I hate my father; I hate those two boys who brought me to Atlantic City. I hate all three of those pieces of shit. It's OK to hate them, isn't it?"

I don't think she was totally surprised by my answer but still a little stunned. "No. It isn't OK to hate them." I deliberately hesitated and then I continued, "Hate and resentment are only destructive to you and your mental well-being. If you want to improve your life, as I suspect you do, you need to learn how to forgive your father and those boys. You don't need to say anything to them or do a damn thing toward them. But it is necessary for you to forgive them in your mind and in your heart."

She seemed to hang on every word, not embracing them, but eager to listen. I asked, "Do you want to hear part two?"

"Yes."

I stated, "It is necessary to forgive *those pieces of shit*, as you call them, because usually in your own mind you also consider yourself to be *a piece of shit*. Am I a little correct in believing you consider yourself less than a normal person or that something is wrong with you?"

Slowly, she responded, "Correct."

"Now I want you to listen carefully. You are a beautiful person in the eyes of Our Creator. The Creator loves you as the daughter that you are and is waiting for you to erase your hatred of your father and those boys before you can be helped. Only then will you be able to erase your personal dislike of yourself, and your current life situation. The Creator and I both can see the beautiful person you are."

She was silent with tears rolling down her face once again. I noticed the bartender and the other women staring at her. Karen stood up and announced, "I need to leave now."

I stood, walked toward her and hugged her tight for just a few seconds until she backed away. I removed a fifty dollar bill I had put in my shirt pocket just in case additional gambling appealed to me. I placed the fifty dollars in her hand and said, "Good-bye." She walked out of the bar.

I exited the casino, and while pulling on to the Atlantic City Expressway my mind hoped Carol would not be too frustrated with me when I told her I spent one hundred-fifty dollars GAMBLING.

Little did I know, at that time, that meeting a perfect stranger would become unforgettable.

HOW TO SAY GOODBYE IN RUSSIAN

By Denice Jobe

"Doh-brey-ah oo-trah," we greeted each other, practicing our Russian. *Good morning.*

It was a bitingly cold November day, a Russian public holiday. Soldiers carrying red flags marched up the street outside our seven-story hotel in Ivanovo. Unlike the contemporary Cosmos Hotel in Moscow, where we'd stayed the night before, the Sovietskya hotel was built in the 1950s and hadn't been updated since. The cavernous lobby, where we waited for the translators, was paneled in honey-colored wood, and empty except for the check-in desk, a pay phone, and a green sofa so mid-century modern it was trendy again. An art nouveau chandelier overhead had burned out. Even the air smelled vintage.

"Spa-see-ba," we practiced. *Thank you.*

The day before, we'd been in Moscow, touring the city, visiting the Kremlin and Red Square, shivering in the sub-zero wind gusts in front of St. Basil's Cathedral to have our pictures taken. For lunch, we ate at Sbarro's pizzeria in what once had been an enormous state department store in Soviet times, but now was an upscale mall. I was surprised to see French fries on the menu, learning over the next several days that French fries are a staple of the Russian diet, served everywhere. Another surprise: toilet paper is not provided in Russian public bathrooms. I had to carry my own supply in my purse.

Raw-cheeked from the cold and weary from sightseeing, we happily boarded a van for a six-hour drive east to Ivanovo, through old-world villages and magnificent birch forests. My travel companions—all in their 40s and 50s—were friendly and fun to be around. Most had been to Ivanovo before; some, like Carol, several times.

"I keep coming back," she said. "I miss the kids."

Everyone on the team who had signed up for the trip to visit Orphanage #1 in Ivanovo had done so for unselfish reasons—to cheer up the children, to make a difference in young lives, to be in mission to others. I was there because when our church mailed us a form asking for help with its programs, I joked to my husband, "Well, I could either donate $20 to the church's operating fund or go to Russia."

"Okay," Steve said.

"Okay what? I can go to Russia?"

"Sure."

"But who would watch the boys?"

"I'll take off work," he said. "We'll be fine."

This is crazy, I thought, checking the "Ivanovo Orphanage Mission Team" box on the form, my head filling with images of Imperial Easter eggs, onion-domed churches and Byzantine art. *I can't just take off to Russia for ten days.*

I couldn't have known then how broken I would be by the time we left; how the impulsive act of checking that little box would be the first step in putting me back together.

We were paired with our very own Russian translators, all of them women in their early 20s, all of them wearing stiletto boots despite the thin layer of ice on the ground.

Olga mothered me from the start, though I was ten years older. "Where is your hat?" she scolded in heavily accented English before we left the hotel. She had a round, cherubic face, limp brown hair, and wore the same two sweaters—light blue and beige—throughout the week. Clothes are so expensive in Russia that people wear them over and over between washings.

"It can get smelly sometimes," Jan, a team member, warned those of us who were new. "Especially in the orphanage. It gets really stuffy in the winter."

The 15 of us—team members and translators, and Anya, our petite, briskly efficient guide—piled into a van for a ten-minute drive to a Russian Orthodox Church to attend Sunday services.

The towering red-bricked cathedral with high arched windows, scalloped cornices and three onion domes topped with metal crosses took my breath away. Congregants, the majority of them elderly ladies in long coats and head scarves carrying tote bags, hurried in and out of the massive double doors. I covered my own head with a floral scarf.

There were no pews inside the church, only a circular, high soaring space with an altar in the middle. Glittering icons of Mary with baby Jesus and religious scenes decorated the walls. Tables around the room were weighed down with hundreds of lit votives. A priest in ornate robes, and several nuns, chanted and sang in Russian, their voices echoing. People in family groups stood in silence.

At first I thought we'd missed part of the service, but Olga quietly explained that it would go on for hours, with people coming and going. The women bustled around the sanctuary, collecting scraps of paper from worshippers, delivering them to the nuns.

"Written prayers," Olga whispered.

There is something about the grandeur of a centuries-old cathedral—the rituals, the incense-scented air, the carvings and stained glass—that moves me, that makes God seem closer. Thousands of miles from home, listening to a sermon in a language I didn't understand, with little Russian ladies scurrying around me, the anger I felt toward God, and the universe, and cancer—and the guilt I carried inside—began to ease.

My mother passed away three months before I left for Russia, and between the time she was diagnosed with lung cancer and died—just five months—we spoke of death only once.

"Isn't it better to go suddenly?" she asked tearfully. "Isn't it better not to know?"

"No!" I said.

At the time I was thinking of my grandmother who had died suddenly, giving me no chance to say goodbye. *Knowing is better*, I told myself. I can prepare. I can say what I have to say. Turns out, Mom was right. Sudden is better.

What did I think we were going to talk about? Her fears? She kept them to herself. Relieve my conscience? There was nothing to resolve. Everything that I'd ever wanted to say to Mom had been said. Talking about the past now made her cry. Making funeral plans meant that we had given up, so we didn't talk about that either. All there was to talk about were her appointments and treatments, the only certain things.

A round of radiation caused Mom's hair to fall out and I'd offered to shave my head in solidarity. "Don't you dare!" she said.

The floral scarf I wore in the Russian church was hers.

The sermon was still going on when we left thirty minutes later. After a short drive, we pulled up to Orphanage #1, a plain two-story tan-painted building. The door flew open and children ran out, older ones throwing their arms around team members who had come

59

before, younger children hanging back, shy. I felt shy myself, stepping down from the van, overwhelmed, uncertain how to act.

In the common room, where all the kids were gathered, Russ, one of the two guys on the team—Scott was the other—led the group in a simple sing-along in English. Afterwards, I had a chance to talk to Dima, an 11-year-old boy with brown hair and eyes, and a sweet smile. The conversation stumbled at first, as we got accustomed to speaking through Olga, but before long Dima was telling me about school and his favorite sport (soccer) and asking me about life in America. Too soon it was time to go, and as the team stood in the hall, saying our good-byes, Dima clung to me like he never wanted me to go, and I looked over his head, blinking to keep tears from falling.

Lunch was at B-mart, a department store with a cafeteria-style restaurant inside. Along with the ubiquitous French fries, the self-serve buffet featured borsch, potato salad and sausages.

Eyeing a pan of flat things in a sauce labeled "cutlet," I asked the woman behind the counter what kind of meat it was. She shook her head, not understanding, so I called Anya over.

"What kind of meat is this?" I asked.

"It's a cutlet," she said.

"Is it beef? Pork?" I asked, conscious of the line getting longer behind me

Anya shrugged. "It's *joost* meat."

Resigned, I ladled some on my plate. (It tasted like chicken.)

An old, gloomy looking apartment building was our next stop. Two 17-year-old female graduates of the orphanage lived there. In Russia, children are forced out of the orphanages at 14, and, if they are lucky, placed in government-subsidized apartments with periodic visits from a "house parent." Essentially adults, they are expected to shop for groceries, do their laundry and cook for themselves, get a job or attend a tech school or, if their grades are high enough, go to college.

I would have been appalled at the rundown condition of the apartment building if it were any different from the hundreds of other dreary apartment buildings in the city. The stairs to the second floor were covered in moldering trash and paint was chipping off the walls. Yuliya's and Nastya's apartment, however, was clean and tidy. The girls flitted around the tiny space, which I could tell they were proud of, serving tea and store-bought cookies. Being motherless myself, you'd think I'd be able to relate to these girls, but the visit was awkward because of the language barrier, and because I didn't know what to say to teenagers who had lost so much, and who were so childlike and hard-edged at the same time.

After leaving the apartment, we met the girls and a dozen more graduates at a nearby pizza place with a party room upstairs—a sort of shabby Russian Chuck-E-Cheese—with cartoon characters painted on the walls and coin-operated video games. A bizarre place to bring teenagers who had stopped being children years ago, but Anya had chosen the location.

The seven team members and our translators split up among the graduates, and thus began ninety excruciating minutes—I secretly checked my watch—of conversing with four teen girls who looked as though they'd rather be anywhere else than sitting here answering my questions—"What are you studying in school?" "Do you have a boyfriend?"—through an exhausted translator, who, for all I knew, could have been telling them, "Sorry you got stuck at this table. It's almost over."

Back in the hotel room I shared with Carol, alone for a moment, I began to cry. *What am I doing here? I can't help these children.* I felt completely inadequate to the task I signed up for. I was in a strange country, completely cut off from my family. And I wanted my mother.

After Mom had been diagnosed in April 2007, I telephoned her every day, like I had before she got sick, but getting her to talk became a struggle. She seemed far away already. It got to the point where I dreaded calling, because I didn't know what to say and she didn't either. For the first time, there were uncomfortable stretches on the phone that we didn't know how to fill. I felt shut out of her life. I didn't know whether to be a cheerleader or listener. I asked her once, what she wanted. "I don't know," she said. "Just be there."

She seemed to be tolerating the radiation treatments well, so it was a surprise when she had to be admitted repeatedly to the hospital, once for dehydration, twice for blood clots in her legs. The last time she was admitted, her legs were so swollen she was nearly paralyzed from the waist down. Those heavy puffed-up legs were especially difficult for her to cope with because she'd always been self-conscious of having chubby legs, and never wore shorts.

Until this point I had lived in complete denial. We lived an hour apart, close enough for me to help in a crisis, but far enough away that I was shielded from the day-to-day realities of her treatment. I would have these rare moments of clarity when the implications of her illness would hit me and I'd fall apart, but most of the time I went on with my life, totally unable even to conceive of a world without her. It was easier that way.

To address the clots, her doctor inserted a stent. He talked about her going home, but she didn't want to leave the hospital. I think she must have known what I refused to accept.

That afternoon, I took the doctor aside to ask, "What now?"

He looked me straight in the eye. "This is it. It's over."

Numb, I returned to her bedside, told her what a wonderful mother she was, but she turned away. "Leave me alone," she said. "I don't have the energy to talk to you right now."

The next day she was released to hospice care at home, where I stayed for the next five days. It was astonishing how quickly she deteriorated. This fiercely private woman let me feed her and hold her while she used the toilet. My brother said later that he felt privileged to have been there, part of her inner circle. She refused to see my husband, my brother's wife, or even the grandchildren. "I don't want them to see me this way."

One day, she struggled to put a pill in her mouth and kept dropping it. "Damn it, what's wrong with me!"

In that moment of frustration, I caught a glimpse of her spirit, as strong as ever, trapped inside. I'd always struggled with my beliefs of the afterlife. But now I was convinced that her soul wouldn't just die with her body. It had to go somewhere.

Mom's legs bothered her, so I did what I could to ease the discomfort, rubbing them, covering them with damp cloths when they burned from lack of oxygen. Hour by hour, it seemed, the purple crept under the skin from her toes, over her feet and up her ankles, like a shadow—like death. If I could just stop it from spreading—make it go away—I could save her.

"Put socks on her feet," the hospice nurse suggested.

I did, hoping it would help, knowing deep inside that the socks were for my benefit, so I wouldn't have to look at my mom's feet anymore. I never realized that hospice was as much involved with helping the family let go as caring for the patient.

"We don't know how to die anymore," another nurse told me. We started out hating the nurses, ended up loving them.

I administered morphine every four hours, and when the drug wore off, Mom would come around. She was sometimes alert, mostly incoherent, looking at something in the distance only she could see. Overnight, my brother and stepfather slept on the couch and loveseat. Both snored so loudly that I couldn't have drifted off had I wanted to. Sometime in the night, my brother woke up, glared across the room at my stepfather for making so much noise and fell back asleep. Ten minutes later, it was my stepfather's turn to wake up and complain, "Could your brother snore any louder?"

Near dawn, Mom sat up asking for a dictionary. My heart beat rabbit-fast as I took the stairs two at a time to the office upstairs to scan the shelves. *What are you doing?!* All I could think of was her downstairs, trying to get out of bed and falling. Grabbing a book at random, I brought it to her. "What do you want me to look up?"

By then she couldn't remember. She started to get agitated; I panicked. I could have woken my brother and stepfather, but that would just add to the turmoil.

"I forgot…" she moaned. I couldn't make out the rest. *What did the nurse say?* I tried to remember, something about just reassuring her.

"No you didn't," I said. "You took care of everything."

"It's my fault…all my fault."

"No, no. It's okay."

I started her on morphine around the clock after that, which kept her in a constant twilight state. I felt like a coward, because I could not say if medicating her was for her benefit or mine, even though the nurses had urged us never to let the morphine wear off. Fluid had filled her lungs, she was suffocating, and the drug helped her relax. We'd resisted, so desperate for those rare moments between doses, when she was Mom again and could speak to us.

Every time I squirted the drug into her half-open mouth, it felt like an assault. I told myself that if the roles were reversed, if I were lying there, I would trust her to do this for me.

The last twenty-four hours were quiet, long-drawn-out. I watched her suffer, helpless to relieve it. We listened to the soundtrack from the movie, *Somewhere in Time*. My brother went home to his family. My stepfather made final arrangements. The hospice nurse bathed her, changed her bed linens, called her "Miss Sue." Her breathing, though quick and shallow, was calmer, because she wasn't panicking anymore about the lack of air. But her body was strained, her back arched and her arms straight. She still fought. I painted her toenails, held her hand. When had I ever been this close to her? Been aware of her every breath and heartbeat?

She died on a Tuesday morning. I was on the phone in another room, talking to my husband. I felt a change. It was so slight.

I knew without looking she was gone.

They say that there is no such thing as time in Heaven. That final week with Mom, it felt like some of the timelessness of Heaven had leaked in, surrounding us. Time passed so slowly. As soon as she was gone, time sped up again, to catch us up to the rest of the world, which had been going on the whole time.

At first, it had been a relief to go to Russia, to outrun grief for a while, to live in the moment and forget about everything. But after the surprise of Dima's hug, the bleak apartment buildings and the disastrous evening with the graduates, sorrow overwhelmed me, and I felt as helpless as I had the last days of my mother's life.

"It's okay," Carol said kindly when she walked into our room. "It gets to everyone."

The next day we took the children from the orphanage to the zoo. Dima saved a seat for me on the bus and held my hand. What a strange, sad little zoo, with its ramshackle cages and outbuildings, and junk strewn around, including an old rusty van. Despite the zoo's neglected appearance, it had two tigers, three bears and a lion. The kids loved it; most had never been to a zoo before.

Back at the orphanage, we played monkey in the middle in the hallway, and decorated t-shirts. I found out that Dima's favorite toys were Matchbox cars, but that these inevitably ended up stolen or hoarded by other children. My sons had dozens of toy cars to play with and this Russian child did not have even one!

The next four days passed in a whirlwind of activity, with no time to think about Mom, or life back home. We had "spa" day for the girls, turning the common room into a beauty parlor with make-up, nail polish and hair accessories. As expected, the girls loved it, and I found it much easier to talk to them while styling their hair in an elegant up-do. We also decorated keepsake boxes and picture frames, had sing-alongs, indoor scavenger hunts, and a board game challenge. To every child we handed out backpacks filled with school supplies, slippers and new pajamas that had been donated by members of our church. As the week went on, I found myself growing attached not only to Dima, but to two teenage girls—Sveta and Katya—who could not have been more different. Fourteen-year-old Sveta was slender, with brown hair and eyes, and a quiet, shy manner. Katya was a year younger and stockier, blonde and blue-eyed, and as rough and tumble—and belligerent—as the boys. Before coming to Orphanage #1 two months before, she had lived on the streets.

For many days the children had been rehearsing for an evening performance in our honor, and the team had organized a full day's "carnival" activities leading up to it, including face painting. For two hours, Olga and I decorated faces with butterflies and flowers, and for the majority of boys, red and black Batman style masks around the eyes. When it was Katya's turn, she demanded a Batman face, too, but eventually chose cat's eyes and whiskers.

The orphanage caretakers were annoyed with us. Here, the children were supposed to be on stage later that evening, dressed in their best, performing traditional dances, and we had decorated their faces! Any child they could get their hands on was scrubbed clean. I felt bad, until later that night, when a gang of little boys in black vests and Batman faces took the stage for a polka. It was a magical evening that brought the entire team to tears.

We only had two hours with the children the next day before leaving for Moscow. Although we were discouraged from singling out children and giving them gifts, I did manage to smuggle Dima some Matchbox cars I'd bought at the B-mart. "Be a good boy," I told him. "Study hard in school."

The girls—Sveta and Katya—stayed by my side, posing for photographs until it was time to go. Without thinking, I took off the ring and heart necklace I was wearing—gifts from Mom—and gave them to the girls. To see Katya—that tough cookie from the streets—sobbing uncontrollably broke my heart.

"Duh svee-dah-nee-ye," I said, hugging her one last time. "*Do svidaniya*. Goodbye."

Don't look back, I told myself as we pulled away. Russ, Carol, Jan—they were all crying, too—and I thought, *How can they bear this over and over again?*

During the long drive back to Moscow, and the flight home, I ached inside, knowing I would probably never see Dima, Katya or

Sveta again. At the same time I felt replenished, uplifted in spirit, as if my heart was knitting back together.

"Funny how I go there to help the children," Carol told me. "But I end up receiving so much from them."

There are lessons we cannot learn without loss. Joys we cannot experience without pain. Grief that hurts and heals at the same time. I'll never forget the suffering I saw during my mother's last days— nothing can erase those images entirely from my mind—but there were also moments of grace. The soft way the light came through the windows at the end of the day. The tranquil, quiet moments we had together. How time—and the world—seemed to stand still.

Goodbyes wouldn't hurt so much if we didn't love.

I ALWAYS THOUGHT I WAS A NEW YORKER

By Patricia Boswell Kallman

I was born and raised in the Allegheny Mountains of Pennsylvania. I fished, swam in the creek, and wandered the woods and fields with my dog. I ate fruit from the trees and rode my bike. I read for hours in a hammock. It was beautiful, and I liked growing up there.

Our family vacations were often to New York City to see musicals, Radio City Music Hall, and the museums. From the first time I visited, I loved it. I loved the rhythms. I felt most alive there. The excitement and electricity surrounded me. I wanted to be there. Eventually I did go there to live, and felt it was my spiritual home. I was not a born New Yorker, but it chose me and I chose it.

For various good reasons, after some years I moved away. But secretly, I still called myself a New Yorker.

My parents lost their battle with death inches at a time. They waged a long, hard struggle to stay in their own home, independent and self-sufficient. They were able to be there on their own and then with help for quite a while. I could barely take it in the first time I arrived with my family and discovered that my mother had not planned any meals for our visit. Then I was in and out often, traveling four hours each way to get there for occasions, hospitalizations, and just for visits. My husband, my children, my brother, his family, our cousins, and their friends stopped by, looked in on, dropped by to chat, and otherwise watched over them. We acquired walkers and wheelchairs, lift chairs and hospital beds, and caregivers for them. Papers were put in order, and we took over their financial and medical affairs.

My father, the can-do man, became frail. My mother, the organizer, could no longer walk, although she thought she would be able to soon. Together Dad and I could no longer lift her. Mom went to live in a nearby nursing home. Caregivers took Dad every day to visit her. My father had an incident while alone one morning before the caregivers arrived. He blacked out, fell, and couldn't walk. Tests were done, while he complained and refused hospital food. When the hospital was finished with him, he went to live across the hall from my mother in the nursing home. When a room opened up, they were to be moved in together.

Dad found food more and more repugnant. Finally he refused even his favorites and would not eat at all. He died at 88 on March 8, 2009, in his sleep with my mother, my husband, and me by his side and the rest of the family on their way.

Mom, my brother, and I made decisions, and slowly got their house ready to sell. There was no big rush. My brother had bought it from them years before to ensure that they could stay there as long as possible. Now Mom understood that she would not be going home, although she did think she might be able to have a small apartment somewhere, sometime. We told her we would put anything and everything she wanted into storage.

When it had become apparent a year or so before that neither parent would ever be able to climb the stairs again in their home, I began to sort and organize the upstairs floors. I often channeled my energy into this while they napped in their lift chairs or once they were in bed for the night, and a quiet evening stretched out ahead of me. I organized photos, drawers, and shelves. Now, I took boxes of my mother's "friends," her books, to the nursing home, and she decided what she wanted to store and what to donate. She wanted me to take all the important stuff, the movies, photos, and scrapbooks, home with me for safekeeping.

One visit, one evening I said good night to her. I told her I loved her and I'd see her in the morning. I went home, to their home, my childhood home. The girls, as Mom called them at the nursing home, cared for her in the early morning of July 29, 2009. They said she had not wakened, but was talking to Dad in her sleep. About half an hour after that she was gone.

A few months had passed, necessities were taken care of, and healing had begun. I could not wish my parents were still alive. They would not want to be. There'd been sad and bad times and some happy times since their deaths. There had been trips with the van to my home, and my brother had taken a van load home to Iowa. I had donated and cleaned. Now I sat in a lawn chair in the living room as an auctioneer finished loading a truck with their things we would sell. We settled up, and the truck drove away. I walked silently one last time through the empty basement, the garage, the house. I got to the front door to leave, and I had to do it again. Another last time. In my parents' bedroom, I started to scream. I was shocked that I was screaming. I sat on the floor of their empty room and cried and screamed and cried for all that was gone. I couldn't believe that it would never be again. Heading home to Virginia, I cried all the way across Pennsylvania. I stopped a few times when I couldn't see to drive. I didn't know if I would ever stop crying.

It took a long time until I realized that everything I was crying for, I would always have there crystal clear in my memory. My parents would never be lost to me. I could go home anytime I wanted or needed. My mind would always contain every detail of that home of my heart. It took me three years until I was able to sit down and write this. For three years I wasn't sure what it was that I needed to write. Now I know what I wanted to say. Until October 19, 2009, I mistakenly thought I was a New Yorker.

I BRING YOU YOUR WIFE

By Rebecca Thompson

He summons. My eyes open. I look over to the dark corner of my
room. I feel rather than hear his earnest words.

Bring me my Nene, my little girl.
Of course Daddy, I promise.
Good night, sweetheart, good night.

My throat catches. My heart aches. He would say that when I was a little girl. A pure, delicious thrill would sweep over me that would make me want to cry. I matter.

* * *

Cold Christmas morning dawns with a misty breath of damp, hazy fog. We go to him. In the gloomy chill and eerie cast, the lonesome dead lay on pristine slanting hills. Silhouettes of gnarly, bare trees frame the somber cemetery, their boughs drenched in dew. Trailing wisps of fog lace and drift low over long rows of tombstones. No one but us visits.

Bundled and bowed, feeble on my arm, she falteringly makes her way to him. My mother's steps are heavy. Old. Reaching him, she stoops awkwardly and her fingers trace the etched name. Drawing smooth circles around his name, she tenderly caresses her beloved. She straightens and looks down at her dewy fingers laced with tombstone grime, with him. With cold wet hands she cups her cheeks and closes her eyes. In a quiet, frail trance she rubs him into her. In steady rhythm, she presses him onto her eyelids, lips, her chin. Lowering her hands, she loosens her scarf and clasps her neck, pushing him into her pores, rubbing deeply. He whispers to her.

Drink me Nene…I come in.

Glow seeps into her sallow, sunken face. She blinks, breaking trance. Doleful, barren eyes fill with a warm gleam. Catching a glimpse of the past, what was, I see her and revel. She filled our pages and spaces. Fearsome mother and warrior woman: seeking, hurtling and restless. Gushing with life, yielding and wielding, she is fire…his wife.

Memories and images flicker, quickly fading. Looking around, I see only this morose, wan woman. Gaunt. Pierced by loss, she is left bereft. I hurt for her.

She lowers to a worn chair, swaying. Catching her, I cover her with a blanket. I hold her to me. Squeezing eyes shut, my chest tightens. I wish for her solace, comfort. At her quavering sigh, I let go. The keening starts. I watch her yearn; it withers me. Stepping back, I give him his
Nene.

She stares at his tombstone. He lures. Tethering herself to his grave, he holds her. He strokes and she is consoled. She is wife, his woman, devoted in life, in death, in the stream of eons. Lost in her

71

mourning, she whispers to him. Her words fraught with worry and steeped with longing. She questions. She hankers. Beseeches. Laughs. Scolds. Whispering like a schoolgirl, her expressions are ardent, petulant. Her tales, lonely.

"Are you in heaven?"

"I would make you coffee…"

"You are happy, yes?"

"Do you sit with me at night?"

Moments pass, the whispering trails off. Spent and wretched, she slumps in her chair. Her little fragile body curls in. I think of a small dejected girl. She shivers, cold stealing into her folds and bones. Her face, ashen. A mewling wind picks up, urging me to worry.

I near the little one. Gently touching her, the moist sheen of her crumpled face moves me. Her eyes open, I fall into desolate pools of ragged, relentless grief. Her hollow cheeks streaked and stained with dirt, with sorrow. Her eyes wail, knowing we must go. She trembles, dreading the emptiness of leaving him. Untended. Alone.

Looking beyond the cemetery gates and the vast swath of purple grey sky, the pulse of the living beckons. I go to gather what is left of her. Straining, I try to lift her. Her body is heavy, sodden with the anguish of leaving him. I cannot move her. Feeling worn and scant, all light leaves me. Grimly, I plead with him. Please, let her go. She is COLD.

A grip eases and lets go. Weaning her from him, I pull her to the living. She stands. Facing him, she draws from within. The tethers fall and she smiles a lingering farewell, lustre in her eyes. As she speaks, I see her. I am mesmerized. She is womanly and beguiling. Soaring strong and steady, she is radiant. His beautiful wife steps closer to him. Palm on tombstone, on him, she whispers:

"I love you, I love you, I love you…."

I cannot speak. Taking her hands, we turn for the gates. Bracing ourselves against the hiss and heave of wind, I hear faint words come from the singing whistle of wind. I strain to listen. A thrill sweeps over me:

Good night sweethearts, good night.

His little girls walk away.

In the gloomy chill and eerie cast, the lonesome dead lay on pristine slanting hills.

* * *

72

THE JOB AND THE DEAD

By Rebecca Thompson

"Dead bodies. Dead of night. Broken glass. Debris everywhere. Vehicle 1, Vehicle 2. Wreckage. Carnage. Saw and felt lots of things like…the dread." Jeff paused. His face sagged, letting out a tired sigh.

Jeff was a policeman for 30 years. A traffic homicide detective and sergeant of a CRU, Crash Reconstruction Unit, for 11 years. This interview dredged up Jeff's memories of the job, victims he got to know (though dead) and the families that cared or did not care.

* * *

INTERVIEWER: How many crashes did you work?

JEFF: 86 fatals and maybe 3 times that in crashes.

You walked up to a scene, what did you think and feel?

It started before that. Way before walking up to the carnage. I'd mark out a couple blocks away. Prepare myself. My heart would be pounding. Was anxious, really anxious. The dread, I'd be overwhelmed by it. Steeled myself against the cold. Had to survive the moment so I could move beyond it. Get back to my life. Home to the wife, the boys. I hardened. Calmed down.

Tell me more about that dread…what was it about?

Many things. Drama. Pain. Didn't want to deal with it. Families, bureaucracy. The media. Flood of questions. The case. Painstakingly picking up evidence. Hated that. Picking up small stupid shit, bagging possible evidence.

The dread. Scared to fuck it up. I'd get closer to the crash, observed from afar. I slowed down - looked to see the entire scene. Was the scene protected or contaminated? Looked for evidence. Direction of travel. Placement of vehicles. Played a movie in my head, watching cars roll and crash.

You got to the scene. What would be going on around you? What did you do first?

73

Took my time getting out of the car. Always had a pen, a small note pad in my hand. ALWAYS.

You say that like it was significant?

That notepad protected me. I saved myself. Had to look like I was figuring, ciphering. Examining kind of thing. Needed to look serious, have the furrowed brow, you know. If someone approached and I wasn't ready for them, I'd look down at my notepad. Scribbled. I'd hold up my finger so they wouldn't interrupt. I wrote. So I could breathe. I was posturing, I suppose.

What did you scribble?

The date. Weather. A car model. Anything to buy time. The duty officer (or in charge guy) and I talked. He had a notepad. Protected himself. Had to save himself too. When he talked, I didn't write. Let him feel important. Allowing him to talk bought me time. Listened. Nodded. Asked questions. Hmm, really? Over there? He repeated, I repeated. Then, I started listening. Really listening. The machine started. Fear subsided. Fell away. I could finally engage.

So you got in that zone, the work mode. The fear and dread was gone. What were your thoughts then?

Had to be systematically unsystematic. If rigid, I paid. Made a mistake or missed something. I was on guard. I protected me. Fluid. Had to be ready to decide. Gave directions. Managed. The other cops, they'd be young, wide-eyed. They got caught up…didn't want to fuck up as well. Some of those young sergeants, they were babies. They think they knew what happened and they surmised the crash wrong most of the time!

Scenes…bedlam. Total mayhem. Two fire trucks, five cop cars, media. Upset, angry bystanders. Why weren't we helping the kid? Why was he still lying on the road? Why has the driver NOT been arrested? It'd take a while to figure out. I've had over a hundred people on a scene.

I'd walk away, get low. Hunker down to the road. Watched that movie in my head. Figured out the first events. Sometimes it was self-evident. Other times, had to figure it out. The guy ran off the road here to the right. He overcorrected, came back to the road, struck the other car and bounced like a billiard ball and redirected. I'd piece hard evidence together. Formulated the events. I liked the theorizing, being a detective. Uncovering. Unlayering.

The victims, the dead, what about them? What were you thinking about them?

They're dead. Who, what, when, where, why and how. I profiled. It was the ultimate profiling. Thoughts went like this: Somebody was drunk. Or everyone was drunk. I was tainted. But when I started to work the investigation, the victims had to be faceless, raceless. Was bound by the creed. I was entrusted to get the facts.

What's the creed?

Looking up…

"No greater honor will ever be bestowed on an Officer or a more profound duty imposed on him than when he is entrusted with the investigation of the death of a human being. It is his duty to find the facts, regardless of color or creed, without prejudice and to let no power on earth deter him from presenting these facts to the court without regard to personality." ~Anonymous~

Felt serious about it.

Back to the victims. What was going on with them?

Most of the time, they were gone. If there was any viability, any hope at all, they were taken to the hospital because it was a medical case. If dead, truly beyond any hope at all, the bodies weren't moved. It became a homicide investigation.

What did you do with the witnesses?

God, they were laborious. If it was manslaughter, hit and run, whodunit, then witnesses had to stay. Woe to the cop who let my witness go. Were the witnesses separated from each other? If not, hauled ass and separated them. If these guys were left together, they'd change their stories. Discounted or second-guessed each other. I wanted, needed the purity of what they saw. They were my check-off list. Validated what I was formulating or invalidated it. Young people didn't give a shit. Or had folks who could barely hold it together. They were traumatized. Weepy. It was ghoulish what they saw, you know, dismemberment…messy scene. It was surreal for them.

How did you talk to them?

Interviewed them before the evidence got stale, vanished. It was urgent to get to the essence. Calmed the witnesses so I could manage them. When they were having a hard time remembering, I had the witnesses close their eyes and watched their movie in slow motion. Got a lot more crucial details out of women than men. Guys were mechanical and dry. Just before they left, I asked them what small details stood out in their memory of the crash. You would besurprised at what I got. Stuff like "The driver threw something out." I'd sweep the trees and find a beer can. Reasonable suspicion stuff, gave me an additional layer to investigate.

If the victims were taken to the hospital, were body parts sometimes missed and left at the scene?

Yes.

Would those parts be taken to the hospital?

Negative. What if the piece was NOT viable? You couldn't use it.

The death notification. It was an awful part of your job.

Yeah. Tough. Had to.

How long did the notification take?

As little as 15-20 minutes. Stuck around as long as an hour or more. For families, it's their first contact with true, harsh reality…loved one is DEAD. Had to make sure they were okay.

How did you break the news?

Had a patent speech. Went to the address. Asked to come in. Asked to sit down. Sat. "Bob has been involved in a very serious crash tonight. He was injured and his injuries were very severe. Unfortunately, he succumbed to his injuries. He did not survive." Most folks went ape shit at this time.

You did it just like THAT?

Look, the bottom line is this: every time you work a crash and give a death notification a little piece of you DIES too. It de-sensitizes you. It's about protecting yourself. You can't get pulled in or you're a mess. The job needs to get done. It's business as usual.

How many death notifications did you give?

Between 30 and 40. Went in twos. Had to be ready to protect ourselves. Maybe. From family. Didn't know…who, what to expect. Dreaded giving the death notification but had to be ready for possible danger. Had NO idea what was waiting.

Danger from their emotions?

You don't know if they were dealing drugs out of the house! You don't know what guns they had! You don't know who they were and how they would react. They might be constrained or they puked, bashed walls, fell down. They've grabbed my shirt and screamed: "YOU'RE LYING! YOU'VE GOT THE WRONG PERSON!"

Family also came to me to be held. Comforted. Would comfort and would watch my gun. At times had to stay. No way, couldn't leave them alone… in their pain. Waited till help arrived. Never knew what the reaction was going to be. It was cultural too.

Different cultures reacted differently?

Whites, Blacks, Latinos. They COULD.

Latinos didn't let me in sometimes. I've had to give death notification at the door and let it eat. Suspicious. Wanted you gone right away. They could be tight-lipped. Had to pry information from them. Latinos hid so they could stay.

One case. Drunk Latino. Wrecked. Pregnant girlfriend. She was bleeding from the head. The drunk was fine. He called his brother nearby. They covered up. They scooped her up and holed up. She missed that miracle hour of treatment. She died the next day. I attended her autopsy two days later. Had a cracked skull. Saw the fetus. The baby was perfect. Fully formed…I got angry on that one. They didn't look out for her. Bastards.

Think about this. Latinos come here for a better life. Guess what, some don't get it. I worked dozens of pedestrian fatals. Mostly drunk Latinos. Crossed the road wasted and got ran over. There was this spot downtown. Two Latino bars across the street from each other. Worked AT LEAST twenty pedestrian fatals there. The men would go back and forth the bars crossing the street at night. Wham! Impact would be so hard. Bodies would fly through the air and land on cars. One lady driver was an absolute mess. She didn't hit anyone but was driving by. TWO bodies "fell from the sky." Bloodied bodies landed on her car windshield. A couple of guys had crossed the street together. She could barely talk.

These men came to America to live their dreams. They get killed crossing a street. (shaking head) What a waste!

You sound angry or did you feel sorry for them?

Both. Good, bad, indifferent. These Latinos came hoping to live better, with dignity.Many of these men came from places back home with no electricity, no running water. From the "mountains." They lived in huts or hovels. Illiterate in their own language. Hell, they could barely speak their own language! Worked their ass off, sent money home. Latinos, they're the hardest working people. They came alone. Lived in basements with sectioned tiny spaces. These guys couldn't read. Had no one. Had nothing. They lived shitty lives. They

77

were lonely and had nothing to do. They worked. Drank. They died here, drunk, on some dirty highway. It was a damn shame. So senseless.

So, how did you notify their family back home?

For some of the victims, couldn't. Tried to find out their nationality. Guatemalan. Mexican. Ecuadorian. Contacted consulates. Gave info I had. Sometimes, it was a wash. They couldn't find out who they were. Nada. No one to notify.

That's terrible. Unknown, unmourned. Go on.

The ones who had wives, families. I'd go see them. Still wasn't easy. Women were nervous. Scared. Scared to see us at the door. Some could barely speak English. So, they're scared, in shock AND they're grieving. That's a whole lot on them. Women wept softly, quietly.

Quietly?

Being quiet, meant NOT drawing attention. NOT getting found out. Reassured them that I wasn't there about their "status." Lots couldn't speak a lick of English. It was three, four in the morning. I had to involve an older child to translate to their mother.

You gave death notifications to children! How could you?

Did it twice. Felt awful. Wasn't right. There's no interpreter at three, four in the morning. Just spent hours on a scene. Didn't know what was ahead of me. You gotta remember, this was 20-25 years ago. The teens were right there. Things were in motion. I, we, couldn't turn around. Couldn't leave. They knew something bad had gone down. These kids would actually become the parent. They translated. The expressions on their faces, having to tell their mother. They were so upset too. It sucked.

You also said "Blacks".

(Carefully) Not "blacks." Black male. Black female. African-Americans.

How did African-Americans culturally react when you notified them?

I'm talking about when I went into the rougher neighborhoods. Had to be on guard. Careful. Alert. Some of the communities… were… troubled. Got calls all the time. THEY DON'T LIKE US. The Police. We'd go in on calls, or just patrolled. Neighbors, bystanders, would come up. Around us. Crowd us. Some watched. Others, hostile. No respect. Angry, even smoldering. What do YOU want? What are you here for? Get out of here! Would have to tell them to back off.

Weren't you scared?

No. That's what they wanted. For you to be afraid. Get out of the car and show no fear. They'll be less likely to fuck with you. Be matter of fact. Mind you, it goes both ways. The cops have done it to themselves over the years.

I didn't respond to their bullshit. Their questions. Why should I talk to the bystanders? Fuck 'em. I was there for the family. Now, if they asked if they could help, I'd talk to them. I'm not saying it was like that all the time. Times we'd come in. Bystanders, neighbors would come around. We'd just say a few words. Calmed them. There'd be no trouble.

Now, dealing with the family. Never matter of fact. Was completely different with them. Showed empathy. The black females, the matriarchs. They'd be grief-stricken. They'd fall to the ground. Screaming and crying.

ALL black females?

No. Course not. What I'm trying to say is the matriarch's grief was everybody's grief. They ruled the roost. The women were dramatic. Loud. News spread quickly. When it was a death, the community genuinely cared. Grieved. Weren't hostile. Well, you might hear stuff like,"So, what did YOU do to help, officer?" but for the most part, they tended the family.

Whites? Let me guess, you're going to say they were dignified?

No. Most of the time, situations had less drama…

That's racist!

No, no. Not racist. It's going into a KNOWN dangerous and hostile neighborhood. Black,white, orange! For Christ sake, I'm married to an Asian!

It's what I've seen. What I've experienced. PUT YOUR OWN DAMN TWIST ON IT! It's my reality. I looked around me; I had to know my surroundings in ALL situations at ALL times. Besides, let's not be naïve. You want to accuse? Talk racism? REMEMBER, IT CAN GO BOTH WAYS! I've been hated because I'm white. A white policeman! You have no idea.

(Silence) Let's move on.

Can you give me details of one death notification that stood out?

Many stood out.

Can you tell me about one?

Okay.

Lauren. Young girl. Early twenties. Seriously drunk. Alcho/sensor read .34 or .36. Going too fast. Car rolled. She was ejected. Typical story. She was busted up pretty bad. Thin, covered in tattoos. Guessed she was probably a wild child. The car had baby toys. She was likely the mom, maybe unmarried. The patrolman helped me open her clothes. For pictures.

WHY? Take off her clothes out in the open?

Remember, this was not just a crash. I investigated a homicide. Had to check for other injuries like knife wounds, bullet wounds. I shielded the victim from view. If it was daytime with a whole lot going on, would've taken pictures in the morgue.

Okay. Of course, makes sense. But, "Wild child"? "Unmarried"? Why would you think that?

Well, she was really young. A lot of tattoos. It was 2:30 in the morning. She was ALONE. She was really drunk. It wasn't her car; it was registered to someone else – possibly a parent. You put these things together. You get a sense. It doesn't mean I'm saying she's a piece of shit!

I DIDN'T, I... Go on.

Saw baby toys. It was sad. Baby lost its mother. I thought, what a shame. The patrol guy and I worked together. Quietly. We opened Lauren up. Took pictures. Someone held the sheet. When I did this part and had to speak, I didn't speak loudly. Spoke in hushed tones, really. Softly. Never spoke loudly. It was rude. Didn't know the victims but dying like that… It's violent and rude. Handled the victims gently, because they've reached their death and I just wanted to be kind. Even if there was no life in them. You had to be, what's the word, sedate. Death is bad. Death is serious. Respectfully handled her. Moved her slowly. Gave her a little dignity, you know.

Cleaned up the scene. Went to the registration address. Nice neighborhood. Affluent. Guy who came to the door in his bathrobe was her father. Dignified. Squared-away guy. Moneyed. When he saw us, his eyes looked like he knew. I could see the woe, the pain. It was almost like he was prepared. This moment had been coming. Behind him, I saw a baby walker, baby things, scattered about. Felt a tug.

I asked to come in. His wife, from the top of the stairs was hollering: "What's going on? WHAT'S GOING ON?"

He led us to the kitchen. Mother was animated. He calmed her down. She sat perched on

80

his knee. Was curious but scared. She leaned forward intently as we spoke. The patrol cop with me didn't say a word. It was all on me. As I spoke, mother got up. Paced. Finished up my spiel: "Unfortunately, she succumbed to her injuries…she did not survive."

Never used the word dead. Too blunt. Hard. Never used "morgue" either. The father's eyes welled. I could be wrong…maybe he looked relieved? Lauren's demons had been quieted.

The mother didn't understand what we were saying. Was wild-eyed. "Where is she? We have to go to the hospital and be with her! What does that mean? What does that mean?"

Her eyes searched the kitchen. Like she was looking for her daughter. She also kept staring at the baby toys. Frantic. Her arms were outstretched. Or on her head. Kept pacing in circles. "What do you mean she DIDN'T survive?"

Father broke in loudly. Emotionally. "It means she's DEAD! DEAD!"

She slumped, all breath left her. Slid to the floor. Let out a terrible sound like a deep moan. I've heard that moaning cry. A few times. It's awful. Awful sound. It's the sound of losing your child. I stared at the little child table in the corner. Red, blue, green. It's weird how you remember things like that.

You know, when they cried like that, made that awful sound. They weren't crying for the now. They weren't seeing their abusing, using daughter. The lost soul. They were crying remembering their sweet two year old. Running around the garden with pink bows on her hair. They saw her at her birthday party. Blowing candles. They made those awful noises because… that was their baby. Gone. Forever.

We stayed longer. The father talked about his daughter. Lauren was a wild child. They had put her in rehab. She got pregnant. Moved back home. She got a job, was attempting to put her life back together. She was trying.

As the father walked us to the door, he quietly asked: "Was she drunk?"

Did you give him the truth?

Told him there was some evidence of alcohol usage. Left it at that. Why be brutal?

Did you deal with them for a while? You know, help them out.

You know, heard back from families. They needed closure. Answered questions. Gave guidance. Comforted. I was their connection to their loved ones. Investigated their deaths. Fathers, mothers who couldn't let go would call. Cry. They were troubled. I listened, A LOT. Always felt that listening was a part of my job. Least I could do. Had folks keep in contact for years. They sent letters, cards, called. But never heard from Lauren's parents.

The closure part. Can you tell me more about how families would find that closure?

There was the Marine father. His 17-year-old son Andrew died. Tragic. An avoidable death. Andrew and two friends were in a Jeep, speed was involved. On a hard stop Jeep rotated. Rolled over to the side. Wasn't belted. As the Jeep flopped over, he was partially ejected. As his body was coming out, the Jeep roll bar landed on his head. Andrew was basically decapitated. Head burst. Sprayed the inside of the Jeep.

What happened to his friends?

Not a scratch.

Andrew's father wasn't available at the death notification. In combat. Desert Storm? I had no contact with him till he called a couple of days later. He wanted to get some items from the Jeep. He and his son had worked on the Jeep together. Well, the vehicle was bad. The firemen had taken the boy to the hospital. I don't know why, he wasn't viable. He was headless, for Christ sake!

I don't understand.

When somebody died on the scene, there were contractors that came and gathered the pieces they found. But that night, the firemen took a dead body to the hospital though there was no viability. They were emotional, upset because he was a kid. They're sensitive you know. They're a bunch of pussies. Anyhow, small pieces of Andrew got thrown back into the Jeep. Like a hodge-podge of parts. On top of that, the inside was sprayed heavily. With brain matter.

I told Andrew's father on the phone that I'd get the items for him. The man was coming over, period. He came to the station. He was a colonel in the Marine Corps. He was strack. Impeccable. Sharp uniform. Tall, striking, he looked the part - a perfect commander of men. The real deal.

When he arrived he was ready to go, get the stuff. As we were walking towards the back lot, I offered to collect the items again. He wouldn't have it. About 100 feet away from the vehicle, I stopped. I couldn't let him see the inside of that Jeep. There was brain, skin, hair.

Blood. His son. The odor.

"Colonel, I respect the fact that you are a Marine. That you fight wars and see really bad things. But you don't want to see that Jeep. It is as bad as it gets. LET ME COLLECT YOUR ITEMS."

The colonel appreciated the offer but said he was prepared. We headed to the car. About 50 feet away I turned to him. "I'll leave you here Colonel. Give you some privacy and time. I'll be back there, available. Just wave and I'll come over."

I walked away and turned. Colonel had reached the Jeep. He groaned, grunted. Half fell to the ground, was on his knees. I ran to him. Helped him up. He composed himself. After he got himself together, his need was urgent.

"I'm getting cleaning supplies. I'll be back to clean up."

"Colonel, we hire people that will take care of that."

"I don't want anyone to see…this. Ever."

He was back within the hour. He wore old clothes, carried buckets, cleaners, tools. He took two hours to clean up his son's remains. I checked on him a couple of times, from afar. The Colonel paused at times to collect himself. He wept as he cleaned. It was tough, really tough to watch that. That was his boy. HIS boy.

(Long silence)

I'd like to wrap this up.

Jeff. I'm sorry. So sorry. I didn't realize how bad it was. How hard it was…for so long. Sometimes you weren't able to protect yourself, were you?

No, I live with it.

When I looked at the bodies, at Lauren, I thought of you Rebecca. All that drinking. Years. That could have been you. I got lucky. When I worked the young victims, the boys, I thought about our boys (puts hand on chest). I'd think about how bad it would be to go to the house and tell you that one of your sons had been killed. (swallows)

Jeff. I…I…

Let's go to bed. Please.

LILY IN BLUE

By Dana King

Eldrick's had a nice crowd for Tuesday night. About half full of the usual clientele, people with more money than was good for them, looking for peers to indulge what would be called perversion if practiced by a lower socioeconomic caste.

The sound system calibrated so you could hear everything your target partner said and still be able to plead ignorance if necessary. She came in halfway through Natalie Cole and her father singing "Unforgettable." A redhead now, wearing an electric blue sheath. I almost didn't recognize her, just the sensation of seeing a person who reminded me of someone else until I glimpsed her aquamarine eyes. No one who saw those eyes ever forgot them.

She sat at a table only big enough for two drinks and maybe a small bowl of nuts, had Eldrick's been that kind of place. I waited until her drink arrived and walked over, sat down without being invited.

"Hello, Lily."

She looked at me without recognition for a couple of beats, then blushed to the roots of what used to be blond hair. "Nick Forte? Oh my God! What are you doing here?"

"Working," I said. "I hope you aren't."

Her eyes flickered to the table, then back. "I don't do that anymore. Not since you came to see me after my mother died."

"I'm glad. Really. Look, I won't stay, don't want to limit your availability. I'm sorry. That didn't come out right. You know what I mean. Like I said, I'm working. A cheating husband job. Lots of pre-nup money at stake. It really is good to see you. You look great."

"Can you stay a minute?" It popped out like she'd been holding it back.

"Sure, if you want. I can watch for this guy just as well from here. I'll get my drink."

"I'm in trouble."

I left the drink. I didn't owe Lily O'Donoghue a thing; I'd always owe her mother. "What kind of trouble?"

"That money you gave me—"

"Your mother gave you. I just delivered it."

"Okay, my mother gave me. I didn't waste it. I got a Master's at DePaul and used the rest to buy into a psychology practice. We're doing very well."

"I knew you would."

She went on like I hadn't spoken. "Someone recognized me. From before. Said he'd ruin me if I didn't pay him."

"Does that kind of leverage work on a shrink?"

"Not usually. A lot of psychologists have pasts they'd rather not talk about. It's why we get into the field. The videos he has are the kinds of things you can't live down. I'd have to leave the practice, leave Chicago. I worked hard for this, Nick. I don't want to give it up. But I know it won't stop with just once. He'll be back for more and more and more. What money I make is tied up in the practice. He can ruin me."

"What was the plan before I showed up?"

She blushed. "Work out a deal for less money…"

I raised a hand. "I'll do what I can. Point him out to me when he comes. Give him what you have, tell him you need more time, and make sure he leaves without you. Wait ten minutes, then go straight home. Now act like you're shooting me down, in case he's watching."

He must have been, moved in before my seat was warm. Almost handsome, early forties, in good shape, nice suit. They talked for five minutes. She laid an envelope on the table. He opened it and counted the money—an amateur, counting it in public—then took her wrist in his hand so I knew it had to hurt even though I couldn't hear anything. I stayed put. He wouldn't do something dramatic here, and she'd only scare so much, knowing I was around.

He stood and I left before he had a chance to notice me, waited outside by the valet station. He led me to an unlighted house in Oak Brook, pulled into an attached garage while I killed the headlights and drifted to a stop in front. A light came on inside. I took what I needed from my car and rang the bell.

He answered the door with a look between confused and irritated. I opened the switchblade I kept in my car's console and sliced his tie off right below the knot. His mouth fell open and I stuffed the tie in it.

"I want the money you picked up in Eldrick's and all the videos."

He made a sound. Could have been, "What videos?" Hard to tell with the tie in his mouth.

I stuck a leg behind his knee and took him down hard. Pried his jaws apart and started feeding the tie down his throat. "I want everything," I said. "Slap the floor when you're ready. Don't wait too long. You pass out and I'll leave you for the coroner." He gave the sign before I could start again.

I pulled out the tie. "The money first."

"On the island. In the kitchen." I nodded that way and he led me to it.

"Now the movies," I said.

We went into a den near the front door. He handed me a jewel box with a disc in it. "That's the only copy."

I nodded toward his computer monitor. "There's a file in there, though. Isn't there?" He didn't say, but he might as well have.

Neither of us spoke while the computer booted. When it finished he moved for the chair.

"I got it," I said. Brought up a command prompt, typed "format c:" and hit Enter.

"Jesus Christ, that's my business computer. You'll ruin me. Who are you?"

"I'm the guy who's coming back here if she ever even sees you crossing the street again. We good on that?"

I mailed the money to Lily. Broke the disc before curiosity got the better of me.

LOST SHOE

By Patricia Boswell Kallman

"Your grandchild drives me crazy!"
My daughter called to say.
Her baby voice comes through the haze;
It seems like yesterday…

"I searched my room; my left shoe's lost,"
My daughter said to me.
"Someone hid it, or it got tossed.
It disappeared, you see."

"Where'd you find the right one?"
With sinking heart I asked.
"Just for fun, look in that place.
That's not too hard a task.

"Check beneath the dirty socks
Piled beside your bed,
Or in your drawers or jewelry box,"
I said with mounting dread.

So we scoured the entire house
And rummaged in the nooks.
Found in an hour a homework page
And several borrowed books.

"Wear your good shoes," I suggest
While crawling on my knees.
"They're too small like all the rest.
Mom, look! I found Dad's keys!"

We never found that lost left shoe
Until we'd bought some new.
Then we found it in a cupboard
In a pot we kept for stew.

My daughter is a parent now
And paying parent dues.
I envy her these days of finding
Hot dogs in her shoes!

THE MAGIC FIRE AND OTHER CAMP ADVENTURES

By Ruth Perry

The memories come beaming back to me on hot summer nights when I look up at the stars trying to remember the names of the constellations. They are the many unforgettable memories culled from four amazing summers working at Camp Manitou as a counselor in the 1960s. Collectively, those four summers influenced the course of my life.

The camp was nestled in the lakes and woodlands of Harriman State Park fifty miles north of New York City. It was sponsored by the Girls Vacation Fund along with other two sister camps. A brother organization, Boys Athletic League, sponsored four boys' camps in the same park. About one hundred and twenty youngsters, ages eight to fourteen, from low-income families came to get out of the sweltering city and experience nature, fresh air and camp activities.

There were five two-week sessions with a three-day break in the middle of the summer. The same bus that transported one hundred and twenty campers up from the GVF Office in New York City carried the other campers back home who had been there for two weeks. The counselors—mainly college students, many of whom had been past campers—were fully committed to providing the best possible experience for each and every camper. We were all willing to go the extra mile to make it happen. Staff came from all over the country and from all walks of life. Usually, if you survived your first summer, you became hooked on camp. In turn, many counselors recruited other students and friends, and a large portion of the staff returned year after year.

I was a freshman at college in Ohio, when one of my friends said, "Hey, what are your plans for the summer? I know a great camp that needs counselors." My hometown of Katonah, New York, was only forty minutes from camp. Pay was minuscule, worse than Army boot camp, yet the experience rich beyond measure. Being a camp counselor not only tested one's physical endurance but also tapped unknown hidden talents, patience, imagination, inventiveness, flexibility and tolerance. The unique summer at camp was hard to explain in depth to outsiders without sounding like you were spinning tales. Camp counselors often bonded and became lifelong friends.

I started out as a pioneer counselor and eventually became a camp director the summer I graduated. In the pioneer unit we cooked two meals a day over an open fire and practiced survival skills: fire-building, trailblazing, setting up camp, lashing, recognizing poisonous snakes, and not getting lost in the woods. I became an expert at making one-match fires and was known for my specialty gourmet breakfast item: eggs in hollowed-out orange rind halves cooked over coals.

The unit had one Indian tepee that slept six, and two screened-in wooden cabins that slept eight with a counselor and senior camper in each. I spent a few summers in a wooden cabin called Colabin. There was no electricity and no bathroom; kerosene lanterns and flashlights were used for light and bedtime stories. The unit was very close to the lake and surrounded by trees. At night frogs and crickets gently serenaded us. Outside the screened window openings the bright stars were visible. There was something innately exuberant about spending the entire summer outside, sleeping in a cabin in the woods with fresh air, and the scent of balsam pines. This is always now the spot I go to in my mind when someone says, "Close your eyes, relax and imagine yourself in a special place."

I quickly learned the difference between things needed and wanted. There were few luxuries. You got up quickly in the morning, threw on your handiest clothes, maybe did something to your hair, and made your bed. You then hightailed up to the wash house on the other side of the latrine to wash your face, brush your teeth and begin your day. There were cabin chores to be done before breakfast. Every cabin was inspected after breakfast, which included making sure the kerosene lantern and potty were both immaculate. If the cabin did not pass inspection, the inhabitants returned to correct the deficiencies. If the cabin inspection was perfect, they would get to go first to an activity following mealtime. This was a lesson in teamwork, and the cabin was as strong as its weakest member. Good behavior was rewarded; whining did not get you far.

Camp had a daily free swim and we washed our hair in the lake on Sundays. Staff had the use of the laundry machines every two weeks, and the use of the shower, sometimes hot, once a week. When you only got a weekly shower and sometimes a cold one you experienced the true joy of feeling really clean.

A bugler began our days with Reveille and ended them with Taps. A rest hour was always after lunch, the hottest part of the day, but seldom did the campers actually sleep; only the counselors. Camp was built around a Native American Indian theme weaving together customs and lore from many different tribes. A huge forty-foot carved and painted totem pole from a tribe in the Pacific Northwest welcomed each camper. Each session started with an evening Indian ceremonial campfire stressing core camp values of Truth, Beauty, Courage and Love. The entire camp sat in a circle around a blazing fire. Again, on the last night, there was an elaborate closing Indian ceremonial campfire.

Counselors were dressed in Indian costumes complete with face paint, and the director and assistant wore elaborate Indian feather headdresses. An impressive fire magically started when the director, Miss Olga recited the words, "Oh great Wakonda, if we have been good campers, grant us fire." (What the campers and most counselors did not know was that special chemicals had been prepared and when the wire was tripped by the camp director, the chemicals would mix together igniting a fire with a loud boom and subsequent blaze.)

It was an unforgettable moment brilliantly amplified on all faces, along with being permanently etched into our camp memories. There was also Indian dancing with flaming hoops, sand painting, the telling of an Indian legend, presentation of camper awards and singing. Each camper received a white candle, and beginning with the camp director the flame was passed from candle to candle. At the end of the ceremony, each person made a wish and blew out the flame. Miss Olga then told each camper to take the candle home and light it at Christmas. I always remember that huge circle with all the lighted candles reflecting camper faces, many with tears. Camp was coming to a close for them.

Between the two ceremonial campfires, there was a full daily and evening schedule of rotating activities. Everyone participated in morning squads of table setting, flag-raising and lowering, and campus pick-up; plus other chores that needed to be done to keep camp working smoothly. Regular camp activities taught by specialists included archery, arts and crafts, dancing, swimming lessons, canoeing, nature, hiking, drama, pioneering and Indian lore. There were cabin overnight campouts in the woods under the stars or in pup tents.

On "Gypsy day" the cook was given the day off, so all the campers and staff evacuated for a day of hiking in the woods and two meals on the trail. We'd return to camp around seven in the evening looking like ragged hobos, with usually at least one camper being carried who couldn't make the last mile.

There were other creative all-day programs built around holiday themes, an Olympic day along with a Backwards Day (when the day began with Taps, clothes were worn backwards, the activity schedule was reversed, and dinner started with dessert). And there were the infamous counselor hunts and stargazing practice, after-dinner favorites. On rainy days we came up with programs that included puddle stomping hikes, scavenger hunts and carnivals with booths in the huge barn. There was always a themed farewell banquet adorned with crepe paper streamers, paper tablecloths, small favors, assorted decorations, a mini skit and a special menu. Awestruck campers would not have been more impressed if they had gone to the Ritz Hotel for a meal.

Music in the form of singing was an integral part of camp before and after meals, during chores and while hiking. There were wonderful camp songs ranging from songs about nature to current folksongs. There were always one or more guitar-picking counselors willing to accompany our singing. I always had some empathy for the bus drivers as the campers sang continuously every camp song they ever learned over and over and over during the two-hour bus ride.

At night the staff got together at Kasoge, a cabin where the founder, Mrs. Kauth, lived and sang songs they were singing on the desegregation marches going on in the South as we worked on special projects. GVF Camps were always integrated. Working side by side with counselors and campers of different skin colors I adapted a lifelong habit of judging others as individuals based on their deeds.

The camp director, Miss Olga, was a strong incredible leader and role model. With a background in fine arts and marketing, she was the most creative person I ever met. That, along with her good humor, positive spirit, love of camping, intelligence and understanding of the needs of both campers and staff, made her well-loved and respected by all. I marveled at her ability to know each and every camper as they came up to talk with her so early in the session until I realized she just called everyone "Dearie."

Second in command and equally respected was Miss Janet, an art teacher from Utah. They worked well as a team and played off each other's strengths. The end of camp was always bittersweet; it amazed me how much a camper could grow up and develop in those two short weeks away from home in a safe, nurturing environment. Our campers were like kids everywhere with curiosity and eagerness to learn and explore once they were engaged by a human connection. To learn to swim and not fear the water was a small but noteworthy achievement in their lives. As was getting up in the morning, making their bed well enough to pass Army standards, looking at a two-inch square of the earth and recognizing all the tiny creatures within it, learning an Indian dance, hitting the archery target, even learning to like foods they had never eaten before or scoffed at before coming to camp. The consistent structure of the day, with adult counselors there to show encouragement and maintain boundaries of what was acceptable behavior, all contributed to this growth.

It broke my heart to listen to some of the deplorable conditions and hardships campers would return to when they left camp. Many lived in the City Projects or crowded tenement housing with their families dependent on welfare checks. They knew what being poor meant: free lunches at school, hand-me-down clothes, empty food cupboards before the end of the month, going to bed hungry, never having extra money for the movies or small luxuries like having a birthday party. Some came from families with one parent in jail or where alcoholism was pervasive, and regular unemployment a way of life. Some campers lived in city shelters. Others did not know their fathers. There was little I could do to change their home life. I knew at camp they had at least gotten to know other adult role models and seen there were other sides of life.

Usually there was at least one camper arriving each session who stomped off the bus declaring "I hate camp, my mother forced me to come." This is the camper who begged more than forty-three times the first two days to use the camp phone to call their mother to come get them. And yes, this is the same camper who cried the most getting on the bus to go back home, who ended up not wanting to go home. And in all honesty, counselors often shed tears as the campers

93

left as if they were their kids. But there wasn't much time for tears because in no time the next group of campers arrived.

Although we knew the campers matured from their experience, all of the staff ended the summer as stronger individuals than when they arrived. To our amazement, we all learned to manage with very little. Staff became cleverly adept at improvising and inventing with what was available on hand. It was eye opening and mind-changing. We all discovered our own personal hidden talents—perform an Indian hoop dance, lead a group of fourteen campers on a ten-mile hike and then set up camp for an overnight stay, sing or act in a Broadway musical—all planned in the collective spare hours after campers went to bed and before the sun came up. We functioned on little sleep and with luck a power nap at midday.

Miss Olga always had the uncanny ability to select a person for something they knew little about and had not a clue how to execute, but with full confidence that they could do it. When she initially put you on some committee or special project you were sure she had made a mistake. Yet, it was experiencing her full confidence in her staff and what we could do both as individuals and as a team, to truly pull off something amazing that enlightened each one of her staff to our own hidden abilities.

It was at camp that I learned that what I did could make a real impact in the lives of many children and the camp community. It was observing the difference I could make daily in other people's lives that fueled my whole being and directed my career choice to the field of social work. I spent most of my professional life working in controlled residential settings where I knew frail and vulnerable people would receive good care and be engaged in worthwhile activities.

At camp I was increasingly given more leadership positions, becoming the unit director and then the director of leadership program at Camp Tawanka, the special counselor-in-training program for senior campers who went on to become counselors. Eventually I was tagged to become a camp director at the neighboring Girls Vacation Fund Camp Talako. The leadership skills I developed at camp enabled me to take on leadership roles in my professional career. In my twenty years directing residential communities I often reflected back on my summer camp experiences and how on many days it was not too different from my summers as a camp director; hiring a staff, training and building a team, problem solving, prioritizing, delegating, adapting to change, forming trusted relationships with families and residents and everything else put on my plate.

My camp experience did not just prepare me for life and work. It was during my first summer on a Gypsy day that I first met another counselor from one of the boys' camps out hiking in the woods on his afternoon off. My friend Kib from college knew him from the previous summer and introduced us. George, who had a warm engaging smile, was tall, physically fit, with hazel eyes and hair the color of sunbleached wheat. I remembered the name and the face and we met again and again. Coed all-camp dances were held a few times each summer. George and I would meet there and talk. He wasn't much of a dancer.

Sometimes we managed to see one another at other all-camp events. Initially ours was just a summer thing, each of us returning to college separated by more than five hundred miles and heavy course loads. After my third summer our friendship had grown, sharing mutual camping experiences and stories about our large families. We were both the middle of five children and loved many of the same things: camping, nature, kids, reading, Italian food and exploring the Big Apple. He had grown up in the projects in Queens and had been a camper along with his four other siblings. Early on he had been selected to be in the CIT program (counselor-in-training) and asked to return to camp the whole summer every year. He credited his camp experience and the mentoring he received from the director and other counselors as major father figure role models in his life.

When he graduated from high school at sixteen, he went to university on a scholarship to study engineering. Because he was in a coop work program during the summers he did not return to camp after his junior year except to visit. He still managed to stop by Manitou to say hello and sometimes come over to see me in the evening after the campers went to sleep. Our favorite spot was a large flat rock on the edge of the lake where we talked for hours nonstop exchanging funny stories about what was happening in our lives. We paused long enough to look up at the stars to identify the constellations and exchange moonlight kisses. It was comforting to know whether or not we were together we would be looking up at the same stars at night.

The turning point in our relationship might have been the night I bet him that I could, in fact, light a one-match fire with wet firewood. He marveled at the resourceful pioneer counselor I had become. We

95

fell in love and kept up during college through phone calls, letters and brief visits during vacations. Five years after we met, shortly after sunrise on the last Saturday of the camping season, we married surrounded by family, friends and camp staff. I wore a simple white silk dress and a wedding veil attached to a crown of wild flowers. The wedding ceremony took place in the community chapel in the woods, a mile from where we first met.

MY GUERILLA POET

By Rebecca Thompson

Poem of Santiago Baldevino Balleza
Filipino Guerilla
February 1942:

CALL TO ARMS

While the battlefield was drenched with crimson,
bullets zinged their serenade of death.
While cannons roared defiance in unison,
my dearest comrades drew their last breath.
Cries of fear rang eerily, chillingly,
from distant mountains, hills and dales.
Mother Liberty bled profusely,
ravaged and raped by devils from the gates of hell.

To arms, to arms, all ye brothers of mine.
To arms, to arms ye vanguards of Freedom;
We must fight and die for a cause divine,
and help save the light for the world and thy sons!

***

From a foxhole in war, Santiago wrote this poem in despair and pain. The enemy had just massacred his parents, brothers and sisters. Grief crushing him, he ran through jungle fighting blindly, bullets barely missed him. He didn't care if he died. He lived. But his anguish was deep, sorrow scarring him forever. He had no family to return to, no graves to visit.

97

Who writes a poem when death is all around you? My father, the gallant soldier, the poet does.

A glimpse into this poet's life... Santiago lived on to marry and have seven children. My father was troubled. His mind haunted and his heart heavy, he lived in quiet torment. He often withdrew from those around him. Though he suffered and struggled from mental illness, he raised us honorably. He placed his children on paths to never live mediocre and timid lives.

Santiago did not know how to talk to his children. In his lonely world, he couldn't connect. As a child, I hungered for his attention and scrambled for approval. I looked for ways to reach him. Eventually I did. Through poetry. Poetry was the gateway to my father's soul. When he recited, he was expansive. Open. Flowing. Santiago could not show his feelings but in poetry, he effused. Imbued with vitality, he was joyful to watch and listen to. I adored the gift of him. For a moment, listening to him, he was all mine. I feasted on the timbre of his voice and was mesmerized. When reciting, his voice and eyes filled with passion, wonder, love! Reciting poetry was balm to him. No secret life to wrestle with. No engulfing sadness. He loved dramatic poetry with power and heart. Courage. Resilience. Magnificence. Enduring Love. Poetry lightened his heaviness, lifted the somberness, eased the quiet, dark desperation; making him what he didn't feel in his life, grand. Fearless.

Standing vigil at his deathbed, I watched my father in his last days. The fear in his eyes deepened my soul. This wounded man lived a hard and injured life. Yet he fought to draw breath every possible living moment. Listening to his labored breaths, he taught me, life bestowed is a wonder. For it, you must fight, you must breathe, you must live.

Santiago, the guerilla, my father, was a poet till the end. His memory in remnants, his body failing, it soothed him to recite his poetry. Maybe it helped him feel brave, hopeful, relevant. Sitting by his side, I was still entranced. He recited Rudyard Kipling's poem *IF*, starting off forceful, and confident. His words rang robust and impassioned, then foundered.

> *"If you can keep your head when all about you*
> *Are losing theirs and blaming it on you;*
"Umm, ahh..."

"You got it Daddy, keep going. Next line is *If you can trust yourself...*"

"Yes! I remember! *When all men doubt you...*"

He couldn't remember the rest. I gently took his hands in mine and returned the gift. Drinking in words he so loved for decades, he listened to me as I held his feeble gaze and stroked his feverish face. Trying not to cry and falter, tenderly I finished the poem he so cherished:

> *"If you can talk with crowds and keep your virtue,*
> *Or walk with Kings---nor lose the common touch,*
> *If neither foes nor loving friends can hurt you,*
> *If all men count with you, but none too much:*
> *If you can fill the unforgiving minute*
> *With sixty seconds' worth of distance run,*
> *Yours is the Earth and everything that's in it,*
> *And---which is more---you'll be a Man, my son!"*

Sleep in peace Daddy, my dearest poet.

POPUP

By John C. Stipa

"I'm pregnant!"

The words came through the phone line as crisp as nuked bacon. At least that's what my brain felt like when my wife told me we were going to have our first child. "I love you, sweetheart," I said, trying to keep my voice calm. "Let's celebrate when I get home." It wasn't until I'd hung up that the nerves hit.

We were both 28 at the time and married four years. She had been hinting that the timing was right to start a family. And it made sense too. Our jobs were stable; we made a respectable wage, had a big empty home in a nice neighborhood in Overland Park, Kansas, the most family-oriented place in the US, and staying home on a Saturday night was no longer considered a failed social life. All the planets seemed aligned. Except for one: me.

It was 1989, only nine years after my father had died from a lengthy and brutal battle with cancer. A battle that had nearly destroyed my mother, three sisters and me. The disease did more than strip my Pop of all his dignity; it ripped from us the dominant energy source that was our family unit, not to mention our primary bread-winner.

For me, Pop's sickness couldn't have come at a worse time. Young, immature, and lacking in self-confidence, I needed a guiding hand to advise me to the ways of the world. How to fix stuff, go on a date, throw a baseball. How to have compassion and integrity, be a leader, make good decisions, take responsibility, and handle adversity. Essentially how to be a man. All the things a father should teach a son.

None of that happened for me. I can blame some of that on the cancer, but not all of it. Even before he got sick, my father never came to any of my baseball games. Baseball was one of the few things in the world at which I excelled. It was my *thing*, my source of identity and confidence. Where all the other boys received instruction and encouragement from their fathers, I was left to fend for myself. He never drove me to my games, I rode my bike. Afterwards, he never asked how I did.

I remember getting a new glove and waiting all day for him to come home from work, being full of exuberance to show it to him, explain how I would apply oil and knead the leather to break it in. When he pulled into the drive, I held my prize aloft asking him: "Have a catch with me, Pop?" He waved me off, mumbling something about being too tired. "Oh, okay," I said, my shoulders slumping under the crushing disappointment. "Maybe later." I tried to fight back the tears, but they were stronger than me. I threw my glove into the neighbor's tomato garden. Yes, I was a child and didn't appreciate that he had been filthy dirty and exhausted from his job as a stone mason; too immature to understand the pressure a father feels to provide for his family. But for him to show no interest in my passion meant he took no interest in me. And there's nothing more pulverizing to a son's psyche than a father's disregard for his own child's worth. It was a point of contention we were never able to reconcile.

So when my wife called with the good news, I pretended to be happy. But truthfully, I was scared. Scared about whether I would be a good parent, teacher, and provider. Scared whether I would be able to do the things I felt my father had not done for me. In the years since his death, here was the first true test of my mettle, the announcement that another life would enter the world. A life my wife and I had created, intentionally and willingly. A life I would be responsible to provide for. I don't remember driving home that day.

The anxiety carried with me to a day or so later, July 21, when we went to a professional baseball game, the KC Royals vs the Cleveland Indians. A chance to relax. Our tickets were down the first baseline, lower level. We went with friends from our neighborhood. There was nothing special about the game itself, but the building angst over my wife's pregnancy made it difficult for me to be very social.

Until about the fifth inning when a batter hit a foul pop up high into the night sky. So high, it soared above the stadium lights, disappearing into blackness for a moment before reappearing. As the white orb descended, excitement rose up all around us as everyone stood in reaction to the ball's trajectory. It was coming right at us! Faster and faster the object plummeted. Hands stretched skyward in anticipation of being the lucky one to snare a souvenir. I took my eye off the ball and noticed my neighbor duck in fear. I looked up again and realized it would hit her in the head if I didn't act. I shifted over. The missile loomed larger followed by a piercing whizzing noise. I reached high with bare hands. And then, SLAP! I caught it.

The stadium erupted in cheers. A fan had made a fantastic catch—without the use of a glove. People nearby smiled. Little boys with open mouths pointed in awe. Strangers pounded my back. And yet I heard none of it. Felt none of it. As if I was in my own little world, a bubble of silence, oblivious to the bedlam around me. And then the electricity hit, first in my core, spreading to my limbs. My skin came alive as if I were on fire. Every hair stood on end. I opened my hands and I realized I had caught a ball, this perfect white… *thing*. And it hadn't hurt at all.

I stared at the ball, so small, so pure, so utterly in need of nothing more than for someone to hold it. Play with it. Take it home. Love it. I cradled it, appreciating the weight, enjoying the smoothness against my skin; lifted it to my nose, breathing in the sweet smell. Somehow it spoke to me. This little white object told me to look up. So I did, into a beautiful night sky littered with stars. And just as if someone had flipped a switch, voltage hit me again as I realized that I had received a sign. For a gift like this, a baseball no less, to fall from the heavens could only mean one thing: it was a message from my father. And his message couldn't have been clearer if it had flickered on the stadium scoreboard: that he regretted his shortcomings and when I needed him most, he was there to reassure me everything would be okay, that I could do this, I could be a good father.

Some twenty years later, he was right. My wife and I have two wonderful daughters. And the popup that my Pop dropped down to me that July summer's evening sits on a bookshelf in our home, next to a picture of him.

THE POWER OF LOVE

By Diane Hunter

A Chinese philosopher named Lao Tzu wrote, "Love is of all passions the strongest, for it attacks simultaneously the head, the heart and the senses." For me, it's been awakened in moments of unexpected circumstances that are so exquisite that they stay etched in my heart forever. It was the power of love that gave me this unforgettable moment.

I was about to become a grandmother for the first time. I received the call I had been waiting for on the morning of November 19, 1992, and raced to Fairfax Hospital. My grandson, Joshua Nicholas, was born shortly after I arrived. It was love at first sight. He was so tiny, barely five pounds. I bent over to kiss him. He had the sweet scent of a newborn. Even the medicinal stench of the delivery room couldn't erase it. It became one of those benchmarks in life that made me feel like I had been created for a purpose.

I ran to a phone to call my husband, Reuben. He was at work as a crane operator in Washington, D.C., and had been anxiously awaiting my call. When I told him his first grandchild was a beautiful little boy, I could hear him choking back the tears on the other end. That surprised me. It wasn't often that he gave in to his emotions-- after all, he was a man's man, a tough guy. The first thing he asked me was, "Is he all right?" I was happy to report, "Yes, he's perfect. He's tiny—one ounce less and he would have been a preemie. His name is Josh." He was anxious to see his grandson and planned to head for the hospital as soon as he left his job.

It was a great experience, cuddling Josh and sharing him with my son and daughter-in-law; but we became concerned when he refused to feed. He was too quiet.

The nurse took him to the nursery and later returned to tell Gregg and Laura that Josh had hypothermia. His body temperature was only 91 degrees. We were shocked. How does this happen in a hospital environment? Josh was put under a heat lamp in the nursery. Laura was told that if he didn't improve, they would both have to remain in the hospital. As the day wore on, nothing changed. Our joy was overtaken with anxiety and fear.

Reuben arrived later that evening, smiling in anticipation of seeing his grandson. He hugged everyone, then looked for Josh. "Where's the baby?" he asked. We explained what had happened. He lost his smile. He said, "Take me to the nursery. I need to see him."

As we approached the nurses' station, I saw a nurse holding a baby and talking on the phone. I got bits and pieces of her conversation. She sounded very concerned. It was then I realized that she was holding Josh. When she hung up, Reuben introduced himself and asked if he could hold his grandson. She momentarily let him have a glimpse, but said the doctor wanted Josh under the heat lamp immediately. She returned to talk with us.

She said, "His pediatrician is concerned about the hypothermia and his lack of interest in feeding. This is probably due to his low birth weight. I asked the doctor for the next step. He suggested keeping him under the lamp for now." Reuben asked, "What's the next step if this doesn't work? Is he in danger?" She didn't offer an answer.

We stood at the nursery window for about thirty minutes. Reuben didn't say a word, his eyes fixed upon Josh. I knew him well enough to know that he wasn't going to just stand by. He was deep in thought when I decided to go back to be with our son and daughter-in-law. They were scared. I could see Laura had been crying and Gregg looked weary. About an hour later, an announcement came over the loud speaker, "Visiting hours are now over." It was eight o'clock. I expected Reuben to meet me back at the room so we could leave together. Ten, twenty minutes went by. He didn't come. I went to look for him.

The corridors were already darkened and eerily quiet. I couldn't imagine where he would have gone. I walked past the nursery and down other hallways, but there was no sign of him. I felt uneasy. I thought, *Surely he must be back at the room by now, wondering where I am.* I retraced my steps. I walked by the nursery. The lights were also dimmed, but something caught my eye. I stood there in disbelief. There was Reuben, dressed in a white hospital gown, sitting in a rocking chair in the back of the nursery, holding Josh. I was incredulous at the sight! His big arms engulfed the little blue bundle.

All I could see of Josh was the tip of his nose peeking out from under his blue cap. Reuben had Josh tucked under his chin while he slowly rocked him back and forth, back and forth. Reuben's eyes were closed and he looked at peace. I didn't know how he got into the nursery, but I knew why. He was praying over his beloved grandson. He was now his "Pap" and he was going to protect him. I stood there for about twenty minutes completely mesmerized. My spirit was filled with warmth I could never find words to explain. There's a saying, "Life isn't measured by the breaths we take, but by the moments that take our breath away." This was one of those moments. It couldn't be defined, only experienced. The nurse indicated it was time to leave. She put Josh in his bassinette. We said goodnight to Gregg and Laura and reluctantly left for home.

I couldn't wait to ask my husband how he had been able to get into the nursery. He said, "I asked the nurse if I could hold Josh. I told her that I would comfort him and keep him warm. I guess I was so persistent, she invited me to sit with him in the back. I held him tightly and asked God for help. I knew the doctors and nurses were doing all they could, but I knew Josh needed more; he needed God's love and mine." This comforted me. I added my prayers too.

The next morning, Reuben had to report to work. I left for the hospital, praying that through the night, Josh had recovered and that he and his mommy would be discharged. When I walked into the room, Laura wore a big smile and for good reason. Josh's body temperature was normal and he was taking his formula. I was overwhelmed as I thought about what had happened the night before. The nurse on duty came in, holding Josh. She said, "Everyone is talking about what his grandfather did last night. I don't know what kind of magic he performed, but it worked."

I answered, "It wasn't magic. My husband prayed for God's help. It was all about love."

...

It's hard to believe that was twenty years ago. Seeing Reuben and Josh together today, one can't miss the special bond between them. Reuben still wraps his arms around him; he still prays for him. He does the same with his other grandchildren—Zachary, Evan and Eliana, always with the same intent. He wants them to know how much they are loved. He's their "Pap" and he's here to protect them. I've never forgotten that night standing at the nursery window. It

105

effortlessly comes to mind over and over again because it was a beginning. Reuben's life changed when he became a grandfather. Through all of life's challenges I've seen that "magic" continue to work. It's the power of love—it's unforgettable.

RAGS TO RICHES

By Mary Ellen Gavin

The last summer of my youth, in the early 50s, will always be unforgettable to me. When I close my eyes I still see my favorite day play out as if it were yesterday.

Teddy's tomato-red convertible cut around the corner and we were heading west away from the Lake. Singing with the radio, accompanying our favorite crooner, we rode with the top down to enjoy the sunny day. Teddy was the best wheelman we knew and I sat next to him ... I always rode shotgun. Eddy Dee and Bobby Cole sat in back. We all belted out the Italian tune with Dean Martin, "THAT'S AMORE!"

The best part of our summer was playing baseball and riding in the convertible. Waving at pretty girls walking home from the beach was another favorite. And when they waved back, we felt like Hollywood stars.

Bobby leaned into the front seat and shouted, "Let's get a gander at tonight's competition."

When we nodded, Bobby yelled directions to Teddy and he dutifully turned down Broadway to drive to the new Italian area springing up in our neighborhood. Not that the Italians hadn't been well established in our city. They already dominated the blocks around Taylor and Halsted. But, recently they had taken up residence in our predominately Swedish-Irish-German neighborhood.

Bobby spoke for all of us when he asked, "Why the hell are these grease balls coming this far away from Little Italy?"

Eddy Dee, the most easy-going guy on the team, threw up his hands and tried to explain, "They're Mediterranean people. They love living by the water. The Lake is like a sea to them."

I said, "Why they settled in Chicago with its freezing winters is beyond me."

Another pop song came on our favorite radio station. While listening, we were left with our own thoughts as blocks of Broadway shops flew by. The owners stood outside hawking their merchandise. They kept shouting to us and pointing to stacks of shoe boxes, racks of colorful clothes and bushels of ripe fruits and vegetables all pushed out to the sidewalk. Any other time, we would've stopped to see what kinda deals we could finagle with the bald-headed store owners. Not today ... it was game day!

Since the baseball team representing Sal's Bar was scheduled to play us in a few hours, it was our good-luck routine to check out their clubhouse before we met up with them on the field. This ritual let us take a look inside their hangout and sneer at any of the ballplayers who might be standing around out front.

The drive-by was our own special spin past the enemy's camp to send a message that we were the team to beat. It had worked so far that season. We were in first place and on our way to the big cash prize. All of us guys wanted that money, but some of us needed that money to get us started in a career.

Teddy took his foot off the accelerator, slowing the engine as he turned off Broadway, heading to the Italian bar. The four of us, sitting high in the convertible, must have looked like giants. We were all big guys, athletic guys, who grew up playing ball in the Lakeview area.

I turned up the radio so they could hear us coming. Kay Starr was belting out her famous torch song, WHEEL OF FORTUNE.

Still, I made sure the music did not drown out the sweet sound of Teddy's dual exhausts ... rumbling low and sounding like a lion's purr.

Two guys stepped out of Sal's open door to see who was pulling up to their gin joint. They were short men, dark with lots of hair slicked back and piled high on their heads. No doubt, they were trying to look taller and cooler in the days of the famous D.A. or Duck's Ass Hairstyle worn by that great actor, James Dean.

One of the guys was holding a bottle of beer and chewing on a toothpick. "Whatcha doin' here, boys?"

Bobby was hanging over the fender behind me. Both of his gorilla arms were practically dragging on the sidewalk. "We wanna wish your team bad luck at the game tonight."

Teddy yelled out, "You'll be playing against us and we're gonna win."

The second weasel, standing on the sidewalk, wore a sweaty red construction bandanna around his neck. He squinted at us and spit at the curb. "You are some kinda cocky roosters. Wanna put dollars uppa where you eat?"

We all split a gut at the dumb way the bastard mixed up his words.

I yelled out, "Hope you're speaking for the whole team?"

He took a step closer, but stayed out of Bobby's long reach. Looking up at us, face to face, he almost looked menacing. "Whatta say we put fifty onna head?"

Teddy grabbed the corner of his windshield to stand up and yell at the guy, "You WOPS better have that kinda dough or it'll be Your Heads!"

"Your Heads!" Our voices clamored behind Teddy's. We were not going to back down. Our team enjoyed a reputation for being the first to throw punches. And, we were not afraid to use our wooden bats either. Each one of us was out to finally win that prize money and we were going to make sure everyone knew it.

When the two Italians cursed us in their native tongue, we laughed and waved them off. Teddy pulled into traffic and the convertible hadn't gone a block when we spotted three dark-haired Italian chicks strutting along the sidewalk. Teddy nosed the convertible back to the curb while we tried to make a play, saying sweet stuff to get them to come over and talk to us.

Checking the rearview, we saw more Italians pour out Sal's door. Their shifty eyes were all over us, but they never took step one toward the red tomato.

We gave the girls our best wolf whistles, low and sexy. Bobby Cole, the dark Irishman, smiled wide showing his pearly whites. With a hint of brogue he cooed, "Hey ladies, you gonna come out tonight and watch us play?"

Teddy hollered, "We'll be the winners enjoying the big party."

I added, "And that party'll be at Randy's Tavern!"

It was no good. The gals stuck their noses in the air and kept walking.

All eyes popped up on the rearview to see if the Italian guys had come any closer. Still standing in front of Sal's, they kept hollering at us with words that sounded like a spaghetti recipe. Those sawed-off runts bunched together like a swarm of garbage flies and threw insults at us that we didn't even understand.

Bobby Cole stood up and yelled back, "See ya tonight, LOSERS!"

Teddy put the car in gear and we were off to Randy's for supper. On game day, our sponsor got the sidewalk vendor who sold hot dogs to stop at the tavern. Vienna dogs with all the trimmings and a tamale on the side. Just the aroma coming off Mo's steam cart made us smack our lips.

The league played twilight baseball twice a week and we practiced on the other days as time allowed from our crazy jobs. I say crazy jobs because decent work was hard to come by in the city back then. The vets, returning from the big war and now Korea took back the posts they had left behind. It was only fair, but a lot of men and women of all ages were let go and forced to scrounge for work.

With all those folks competing for jobs, the rate of openings was zilch. Most of my teammates worked two or three jobs ... dead end jobs, part-time jobs, jobs that no one wanted. Jobs that demanded hard work for little pay.

The four of us felt lucky to be able to play semi-pro baseball in a league that was popular in the city and put bucks in our pockets. Just like the big league franchises, the local bar and tavern owners spotted our league fees and paid for our equipment and uniforms. Sponsors were not obligated to pay us, but if we won a game our benefactor slipped each of us twenty bucks. If we didn't win, we got nothing but sour looks, which meant we did not go back to the tavern after a loss.

Our team played for the joint located at the corner of Belmont and Racine. Randy's Tavern was a rowdy place. Two or three fist fights broke out every night. When we were there, Randy looked to us to toss the bums out on their ears.

Randy's payback as a benefactor was the high-stakes betting done privately between the sponsors. Better yet, the taverns and bars made book with their patrons on each game or the players' standings. This side betting brought in serious dough; earnings that were never reported as income. Big money ran through their fingers, but not through their cash registers. Everyone in the city loved baseball and they loved to bet on their favorite local team and their favorite local players.

I gotta say, it was almost like being in show business for us guys. Walking in the tavern after a big win was heaven and made us feel good.

Randy's Tavern had a corner entry that looked kitty-corner across to the Bel-Ray Hotel. This was the old flophouse where the carnival freaks stayed while performing each summer at Riverview Amusement Park. Many a night we got to laugh seeing the fat man taking up two stools at their bar.

Belmont Avenue was the main drag through our neighborhood. It ran east to the upscale harbor at Lake Michigan where the rich and famous languished on some of the finest watercraft built by man. We heard that often those beauties never left the dock to sail out on the lake. Imagine that!

The city was a great place to live back then. We could walk to Wrigley Field and a few miles west of Randy's was that giant amusement park sprawling along the Chicago River at Belmont and Western. During the cold winters, we often dreamed of Riverview's high rides, especially the wooden coasters. I can still hear the chains, clicking one at a time, as they pulled each car up the first rise.

Eddy was our worry-wart ... always reminding us how some riders fell out from standing up and not holding the bar. "You know the park keeps it hush-hush!"

Bobby always agreed with Eddy, "Pounding down those hills at a hundred miles an hour and not holding on? That's a one-way ticket to St. Joe's."

Whenever that graveyard at the west end of Belmont Avenue was brought up, I felt a chill run across my shoulders. Although I had never been there, ducking out of all funerals after the Mass, my folks told me it was waiting for all of us.

The fellas never talked about dying. We were too busy trying to break away and get on with our adult lives. On that, all four of us agreed. Bobby Cole, Teddy Johnson, Eddy ... whose French last name was so full of syllables that it was impossible to pronounce. We just called him Eddy Dee. And, there was me ... Delmar Olson. Two Swedes, a Celt and a Frog. We were close like brothers and we were the iron backbone of our winning baseball team.

An unfamiliar song began to play on the radio. Teddy reached for the volume and hollered, "Hey, this is that Louis Prima tune I told you guys about." He turned it up and we listened. It did not take long for us to pick up the words. Driving over to Randy's, we sang our hearts out to JUST A GIGOLO!

When it ended Eddy Dee proclaimed for all of us, "We love that tune!"

Bobby Cole nodded. "I hate the damn eye-talians for moving in on us, but I gotta say I love their music."

I had to add, "And we love their pasta and pizza pies?"

Teddy agreed, "How did we ever live without red grease?"

We turned the corner at Racine because Teddy liked to park on the side street, away from the traffic on Belmont Avenue, for fear his car would get hit. We got out and saw Mo and his cart in front of Randy's. Poor man was working like a one-arm paperhanger filling cardboard boxes with hot dogs all covered with chopped onions, green relish, summer slices of tomato and a long dill pickle.

The old man saluted us as we walked past and Bobby grabbed one of the boxes that had to contain twenty dressed dogs rolled up in waxed paper. The late afternoon crowd cheered as we walked through the door. Although thinking back, their exuberance was probably more for the hot dogs than for their team members. Bobby grabbed a few dogs for us before he slid the box across the bar.

I motioned to the bartender, "Hey Red, can you give us a lineup of Cokes?" I wanted to make sure Randy's new barman understood there would be no alcohol served to my team until after the big game.

"Sure thing, Del, coming right up." He gave me a knowing wink.

The three tables were full of babes who just got off work at the factories. It was still a wonder to us guys how females in our state could drink at eighteen while males had to wait to be twenty-one. Who said they matured faster than us?

We grabbed the back end of the bar to huddle and had no sooner sat down when the rest of the team burst in carrying another steaming box from Mo's cart. Everyone turned to cheer for Lou Bradley our all-around good ballplayer, Mike Smith who was lean and fast, and the Harrison Boys who dominated an outfield.

All three of the Harrison Brothers; Hal, Hank and Harmon, watched out for each other and the ball coming off the bat. As the catcher and team captain, I never had to bawl out a teammate. If anyone erred, another player corrected him.

112

Mike sat next to me and asked, "Del, what's our strategy for tonight?"

Bobby shouted, "Kill the Romans!"

It hit me that Sal's team of Italian fellas could be considered lineage to the Romans. I stood and the half-filled tavern turned silent. "If they are Sal's Romans," I looked at all our fair skin and blue eyes, "we must be Randy's Vikings!"

The tavern crowd and my teammates went wild, stomping on the floor and howling at the ceiling. It took all my energy to stop the cheering. By the time they quieted down to finish their meal, it was time to go and change into our uniforms.

Leaving the tavern, I stood on the corner and watched each player take off until it was down to me and Teddy. The two of us walked the short block to our houses next door to each other where we grew up like brothers. An hour later, we stepped out in uniform with our shoe bags slung over our shoulders.

Bobby and Eddy were waiting at Teddy's car. As always, we stayed quiet on the drive to the game and listened to the radio.

Pulling up to the field, we saw the rest of our guys throwing the ball around. When they spotted us getting out of the car, they knew to come over so they could help carry our equipment and talk-up our game plan.

Eyeballing the other team's players, the Harrison Brothers sputtered over each other trying to talk. Their separate words finally came out in one sentence. "Do you see those midgets?"

Teddy said, "We supposedly played their team before, but I don't recognize any of them. They must've changed their entire roster. Is that even legal?"

Bobby looked worried. "It'll be damn hard to pitch to them."

Lou Bradley laughed, "Yeah, but our hits will fly high over their fingertips.

Mike laughed, "This game should be a cinch."

Eddy shook his head, "Don't count on it, fellas. They fought hard to get here, the same as us. We got a battle on our hands."

Mike Smith turned to me. "Del, what do you think?"

"Let's feel them out the first inning. If they try any tricks, we'll warn them to lay off or go home with broken bones."

When the game official walked onto the field, we ran over to face him and our competition. My guys didn't know it, but Randy had given me five twenties to slip to this old umpire. I had met up with Tom Larson the week before to ask if he could arrange to officiate at our game. Everyone knew better than to ask him to make dirty calls in our favor because Tom wasn't that crooked.

What we wanted was his favor on the "iffy" plays where no one could fault his decision, one way or the other. Close games are won and lost by close calls. When we met, he did not respond one way or another. But, he did say he was looking to retire and ... he did accept the cash.

While Ump Larson was giving his pep talk, my eyes wandered to the two sets of stands. Our boards were empty. We kept family and girlfriends away on purpose. Our games usually turned into bloodbaths. The only ones who might show up around the seventh inning were a few of the tavern cronies. They were sent to report back to Randy, but that was it.

The Italian stands were loaded with tiny people who all looked alike. They were using their hands to talk and eat food from their baskets. At the same time, they kept screaming their Italian phrases to their team members ... even before the game got started.

Tom Larson checked his notes for our names. "Okay, Del and Nunzio, it's time for the team captains to throw the bat." As he spoke to us, it hit me that Nunzio was the slick fella outside Sal's Bar wearing the red bandanna.

The ump tossed the Louisville Slugger into the air, and because I stood a foot taller than the opposing captain, I easily reached up and caught it. My meaty grip held it about a third of the way down. As we went through the traditional hand-over-hand, we locked eyes until my hand wrapped around the top of the bat leaving Nunzio no wood to grab.

Tom Larson nominated me winner by asking, "Okay Del, ups or downs. Your choice?" There was no choice; we always chose last up to bat.

Randy's Vikings took the field and looked great in our new white and blue jerseys. Our team threw the ball around and began to talk-it-up out there as I put on my chest protector and pulled down my metal-screened mask.

Bobby Cole took the mound and I trotted out to him. We went over our new signals. When he seemed comfortable, I returned to squat behind home plate and catch his warm-up pitches.

114

Their first batter, the tallest of their team, took a few practice swings in front of me. I tried to cover up the fact that my legs were stiff and my knees kept cracking every time I jumped up to throw or crouched down to catch.

It pained me to admit that at twenty I was becoming too decrepit for this game. It was time for all of us to win this pot of gold and go after our main ambition: get accepted on the city police force. With the winning money in our pockets, we could make the necessary payoffs to assure a place on the rookie list.

Ump Larson's heavy hand settled on my shoulder and I turned over the ball to him. He showed me the roster and pointed to where Lou Bradley had filled in our batting lineup. I took a long look at the opposing team now sitting on their bench, according to their batting lineup. I committed each face to memory. They would not be able to change up batters on me.

The old man drew in a long breath and shouted the opening game call from the bottom of his lungs. "PLAY BALL!"

Their first man stepped up to bat. I signaled to Bobby that it was his call on how he wanted to pitch to this batter. Bobby fired a perfect ball that flew above the swing. The sweet sound of it hitting my mitt made me smile.

"Strike ONE!"

All our guys on the field continued to chant, "Hey batter, batter, batter!"

I stood up to return the ball to Bobby and caught a sly grin on his face. He was standing high on the mound and his stance looked as good as any big leaguer.

The umpire and I dropped down for the next pitch. Again, the loud chatter erupted from the field, demanding the batter swing at Bobby's pitch coming in fast.

"Strike TWO!"

This seemed too easy. Where was their long hitter, their player who could hit the ball far and high so he could hustle to second base?

Bobby leaned back and went into his third windup. The perfect ball was nestled in my glove before the swing.

"Strike THREE! You're OUT!!"

My team was now shouting with glee, "Easy Out! Easy Out!"

I kept my mouth shut. Something in the back of my head told me we were going to battle these men for the win 'cause nothing comes easy.

As their second batter came up, I tried to quiet my concerns. This fella was shorter than the first. He couldn't have been more than five feet tall. When he bent over the plate to ready himself for the pitch, I swore he lost a few more inches.

Dropping down behind him, my glove almost touched the ground. I signaled to Bobby, telling him to go slow and low. Too late, his fast ball came in at the same level as his first pitches ... way too high for this batter's strike zone.

Thinking the batter was going for it, I felt relieved. But, he checked in time.

"Ball ONE!"

I stood up, returning the ball and giving Bobby the same signals over again. He nodded and tugged at the bill of his ball cap which was our signal that he agreed. If he agreed with me, why the hell did I see the same pitch cross home plate ... again?

"Ball TWO!"

Balls THREE, and then FOUR, piled up before I could spit. We all watched the short fella skip off to first base amid cheers from his teammates and fans.

I pulled off my mask and told old man Larson that I needed a time out. When he granted it, I slow-walked out to the mound with all eyes on me.

Bobby knew I was mad. He looked away and chewed his bubble gum even faster. "Sorry Del, the little stinker stands so low to the ground. It's hard to find the few inches between his shoulders and knees."

I gritted my teeth, pretending to smile. "Listen, Bobby, you're throwing too high and you know it. Come down off the mound and slow down. A late release should give you a perfect pitch." When Bobby nodded, I knew he was ready to try again and I went back to my position.

Mike Smith, a solid second baseman, stood on the baseline between second and first watching for our prearranged signal. I gave it to him by pretending to swipe dust from my left shoulder.

As I crouched behind home plate the umpire called out, "One Out and A Man On First. Let's PLAY BALL!"

The third batter was a hair taller than the last, but his legs were shorter which lowered the strike zone. I motioned to Bobby with my mitt where he needed to make the pitch and he tugged on his hat to let me know he understood. Standing lower on the mound, Bobby took it slow and practically tossed the ball.

As soon as it took flight, Mike began to do his gazelle dance, jumping into the air and waving his arms. All eyes were on him, including the batter's as the ball sailed inside the strike zone and snapped into my glove.

"Strike ONE!"

I threw the ball back to Bobby. He caught the return and quickly sent it to Teddy, the baseman standing alone at first. The runner had crept halfway to second and was now caught between the two basemen. Mike was moving in on him. When Teddy threw to Mike, he caught the ball and ran up to tag the runner off base.

"He's OUT!

My team chanted, "Two Outs, One to GO!"

It was time to turn our attention on the man still at bat with a strike count on him. I signaled to Bobby to use the same pitch. He went into all kinds of hand gestures that did not mean a damn thing, but looked impressive. When he finally pulled on the bill of his hat, I crouched down and waited.

That's when the batter fell faint to the ground. Umpire Larson and I looked at each other. Neither of us knew what to make of the limp body laying across home plate. Bobby raised his arm to show us the ball. It was still in his hand, proving there could not have been an injury from a wild pitch.

Looking down, I could tell the man was pretending to be passed out and this was a con. Before I could pull off my mask and show my disgust to the umpire, Nunzio and a few of his men were already dragging the batter away.

Larson turned to Nunzio, "Ya got a substitute batter!"

I reminded the umpire, "The sub will have a strike against him, right?"

The ump nodded and called their fourth batter up to the plate. Although, this guy was short ... he was also wide. The man had to be their cleanup hitter, but there was no one on base for him to bring home?

As the umpire and I crouched low, I didn't signal to Bobby. I wanted to let him decide the pitch and he threw the same slow ball as the last time. Mike didn't do his chicken dance because we never used that trick twice in a row.

The pitch was rolling in so slow that I thought the ball was going to plop down on home plate. The bat came under the ball in slow motion and connected, sending the ball up in the air where it caught a Lake Michigan breeze. Flying high, the ball took off, heading for the outfield.

Tom Larson was screaming behind me, "Going, Going, Gone!" He yelled to the batter still staring into the sky, "Go run the bases. You hit a home run."

Dirt flew up at me from the batter's spikes as he sped off. I pulled off my hat and threw it to the ground. My guys knew what to do and gave fair warning to this runner as he passed each one. This was war!

When I saw that the umpire wasn't paying attention to the runner making his way from third base to home plate, I trounced on top of his foot. The little Dago yelped like a dog and hopped away. Their team and fans swore at me and made hand gestures that were foreign to all of us. We threw fists back at every last one of them. They could easily understand our meaning.

Bobby struck out the next batter, leaving their team with one run on us at the end of the first inning. We huddled on the bench while they took over the field to throw the ball around.

Wiping the dust and sweat off my face I told our guys, "Don't take chances. It'll be easy to get hits off them. Let's take the bases, one at a time if we have to!"

All three of the Harrison brothers were close to seven feet tall and they were first up to bat. Our lineup put me last behind Bobby since we were the defense, holding the line on the other team's plays. Working hard while the opposing team members were up to bat, we needed the few extra minutes of rest.

I looked at Sal's team out on the field. They were jumping around like little monkeys. To make it worse, their jerseys were designed in the flag-of-Italy colors: red, white and a crazy shade of vomit green. No wonder the Roman Empire fell ... they must've been color blind.

Hank was up to bat. He stood tall, with his bat over his shoulder while Nunzio pitched a couple of warm-ups. Every throw was wild ... too high, too low or outside. Trying to find the strike zone inside Hank's long proportions somehow flustered their pitcher. He tried, but could not do it. Now it was payback time ... time for us to roll in some runs.

When the ump ordered us to play ball, their second baseman called out to Hank and gave him the finger. We didn't have to be Italian to know what that meant. Hank connected on the first pitch. His mighty swing got under that low pitch and sent the ball flying high into centerfield.

Hank took his sweet time rounding the bases cause there was no need to hurry. When he spotted the umpire looking up, still searching the sky for the ball, Hank stomped on the first baseman's foot and then he stomped on the bag. Looking ahead at second, Hank shook his fist. The second baseman made another unknown hand sign. When Hank ran up to the wise guy, he planted a stinger at the top of the man's throwing arm. The Italians in the stands went nuts, screaming and hollering.

We had no pity for this or any other team. It was understood that we were out to win and take the big cash prize. They didn't have a chance, so I had no sympathy for any of them. This league played rough. Every man had been warned when they signed up that there could be injuries.

That was the last time we made a run. Through a comedy of errors, we could hardly get a man on base. And we fought hard to hold down the other team during the next seven innings. The score was one-up as we went into the ninth.

Anyone could see that our pitcher, Bobby, was tired. Who wouldn't be after putting in a twelve-hour shift down at the railroad yards knocking bums out of boxcars? Bobby wanted a better life. Ah hell, we all wanted a better life.

I pulled my mask down after catching a few warm-ups and gave Bobby our hand signal that meant it was time to win this ball game. The first batter of the ninth stepped into the box and Bobby struck him out ... one, two three. He did the same with the next batter, but the third man up liked Bobby's fast pitch and sent it out of the ball park.

119

Ump Larson mumbled so only I could hear, "Two to one, Sal's favor." We all watched the hitter tag the bases as our outfielders searched for the ball.

Poor bastard rounding the corners didn't spare the horses. He tried to speed past our basemen, who kept one eye on the ump and one evil eye on the small torso whizzing by. Coming from second base, I caught the runner looking scared. He saw me standing tall at the plate and his tiny feet ran even faster until he barreled past third. Right before my eyes, he dropped his back end to the ground and surprised us all by sliding into home plate ... feet first.

Umpire Larson had to use both hands to clear the dust away from his face before he could scream at the runner. "What the hell did you do that for? Nobody was going to tag you!"

I squinted down at the piece-of-crap looking up at us and spit on the ground an inch from his head. "Yeah you stupid idiot, why do you have to show off? You already had the run!"

But, the jerk could only smile up at us because he did not understand a word we were saying. He simply got up and trotted back to his bench. That little trick energized our guys. His team got to watch us dominate over their remaining batters. We made sure they did not score another run.

When we huddled on our bench I said, "We need two runs. One to tie it up and one to take the game. Can we do it?"

Mike Smith smiled, "I'm up first and you can count on me, Del!"

I looked over at Teddy. "What about it ... can you do it too?"

"Sure Del, we're gonna win that money. I promise."

I sized-up the miniature players as they threw the ball around. They didn't look so sharp. Their uniforms were full of mud spots and streaks of blood from the variety of hits they caught when the umpire wasn't looking. Half of them were rubbing sore arms, feet or cramped legs. The other half could hardly see through their swollen eyes. I wondered if any of them had an arm left to throw or catch.

Bobby saw me taking inventory of their bruises and gave me his silly grin. "If you was to ask me why those guys have so many lumps and bumps? I'd have to say they're just too damn short to play baseball."

I laughed so hard that I had to stand up to catch my breath. We all laughed and kept laughing. "Ah Bobby, we're getting too old for this game!"

Bobby patted my back and smiled, "This is our final run. So let's win."

The umpire put the ball into play and called out, "It's the bottom of the ninth. Two To One, Sal's Favor!"

Mike was true to his word. He batted a ground ball that got him to first where he danced around the baseman. He kept it up and everyone watched him sneak off the base and go halfway to second before running back to tag first again. It drove the baseman nuts.

Sal's fans kept yelling at Nunzio to throw the ball back to first when Mike was off base. And, I'll have to say he did try three times, but Mike was too fast. And every time he returned to first, Mike made sure he stomped on the baseman's foot or kicked his shin ... all by accident of course.

Nunzio looked tired and soon gave up trying to catch the runner off base. He turned his attention on Teddy waiting in the batter's box. When Nunzio leaned back for the pitch, I could tell that his throw was going to be lousy. Teddy used his head and let four crappy pitches go by without taking a swing. When ball four was called, Teddy smiled back at me and took the walk.

Mike advanced to second base and was in his glory. He kicked the second baseman while doing his routine again. Wing-flapping and chicken scratching, he teased the pitcher and Sal's guys in the field. Mike's antics forced all their team members to focus on him.

Sal's fans were going crazy over Mike's chicken strut. They wanted to quarter and fry him in hot garlic grease which only spurred Mike on even more. If there was one thing that Mike Smith loved ... it was an attentive audience.

Their catcher called a time out and walked out to the mound. All eyes watched the two men argue in their native tongue. We figured that he was telling Nunzio to ignore our antics and concentrate on the strike zone. Even though they were speaking in Italian, the body language of baseball remains universal.

Lou was up to bat and the catcher's pep talk to Nunzio didn't work. Lou got a walk to first, moving Mike and Teddy. With the bases loaded and no outs, Bobby stepped up to the plate. He knew what he had to do, but he kept swinging at the ball and struck out just the same.

It wasn't Bobby's fault ... he was dog-tired and aggravated. I patted his shoulder when I walked past him on my way up to bat.

Their catcher had a bad mouth on him. He and I had tangled the last time I was up to bat. He liked to lean forward and whisper personal slurs to make batters swing wildly. Too bad his insults came out in broken English or they might have hurt our feelings. So when he tried to call me a 'tree full of squirrel crap' I had to laugh. Kissing my bat for good luck, I growled at him to back off.

The first pitch left Nunzio's hand and stalled right in front of me. It hung in the air just waiting for my swing. My hands slid back on the bat and I let it connect. The ball took off like a rocket and so did I. My knees screamed with pain as I dug my spikes into the dirt. Holding my breath, I kept my eyes glued on the guy waiting at first. He was cupping his eyes, looking toward center field. I didn't care where my ball was headed. All I wanted to do was get my toe on that bag.

The damn idiot crowded the base with his glove up in the air, pretending he saw the ball on its way to him. When my body slammed into him I yelled, "Get out of my way!" He stepped back and I stomped my foot on the bag. I took a look at second. Teddy wasn't there and still no ball. I took off, huffing and puffing.

The second baseman turned his back to me and put his glove in the air. Still no sign of Teddy trying to return, so I kept going to second. The ball and my body smashed into the second baseman at the same time. He fumbled the catch and the ball dropped to the ground. I was called safe.

Standing on second, I looked around the diamond and realized that Mike had been called out at home plate. It figured that Sal's team would go after him, the runner in, instead of me or Teddy.

When the catcher turned around to argue with the ump about the call at second, we let loose and the fireworks began. Teddy and the third baseman were mixing it up. My fists whaled on the second baseman until their fans screamed to the umpire to pay attention. The safe-at-second held. It was an iffy call and old man Larson cashed in Randy's paycheck.

Hank was up again and I had no doubt that his mighty swing could bring me and Teddy home. Hank liked the first pitch and we heard his bat crack. The ball was going so fast that none of us saw it fly to right field. Home run!

The game was over and WE WON!

My leg muscles were so cramped that I could hardly hobble to home plate where all our guys were jumping up and down. They grabbed me into their arms and we shouted compliments to each other. It was such a great moment for us and we wanted it to last.

Breaking the circle, we saw the field emptying out except for their captain, Nunzio. He kept walking around slowly, picking up the last of their equipment. His steely eyes looked over at us until Teddy hollered out, "What're you looking at?"

Nunzio snarled back, "Don't think this is over ... cause it ain't."

Bobby hollered, "We won and that's all that counts."

The little man made a hocking noise and spit. "We'll see about that."

Teddy gave it right back. "Figures, you're a sore loser!"

We all joined in to repeat the childish rant and kept it up as they started for their cars.

Eddy Dee said, "We should probably give those guys a break. They lost a lot of money today and can't even go back to Sal's Bar for a drink. What do ya say?"

I slapped my buddy on the back. "Eddy, you're the nicest guy I know, but you gotta know we can't take any crap off these Italians or anyone else who tries to muscle into our neighborhood. The minute they think we're weak, they'll be out to kick our ass and steal our money."

The Vikings, as I've always remembered my team, echoed my sentiments as we gathered our equipment and walked slowly to the cars. When we spotted the key scratches on Teddy's red paint, there was no doubt who put them there. Teddy got hot! He threw the bat he was carrying up in the air. As tired as we were, we all scrambled to duck the wood as it plunged back and bounced on the grass.

"We'll get Randy to take care of your paint job. Don't worry." I tried to soothe Teddy's anger. "Let's get back to the tavern. There's a party waiting for us."

Our two-car parade honked all the way. Guys in cars or gals walking the sidewalks smiled and waved back. Seeing our dirty uniforms, they had to figure we won a big game. We should have been feeling on top of the world, but I could sense the anticipation we all felt about where our lives were headed.

Since we were not going to be playing ball in the league anymore, we tried to blow off any sadness. And since we would be wearing the badge and uniform soon, we knew we could handle anything those punks could deliver.

Bobby suggested, "Let's forget about Nunzio and his midgets. They'll soon be busy fighting with the next team that whips their ass."

Pulling up in front of Randy's Tavern, we saw the victory signs all over the corner. They were plastered on the outside of the windows and draped over the mail box. Young guys like us, who grew up poor, didn't get a lot of fanfare. We reveled in it. Jumping out of the car, we shouted so loud the whole neighborhood could hear us. "We are the champs and the champions are home!"

Cars pulled up behind us with the rest of the team. We all basked in the glory. Flash bulbs popped in our eyes as we walked through the door. Our girlfriends waited at the bar and kept smiling as they took our pictures.

Vivienne Nelson, my childhood sweetheart from Hawthorn Grammar School, put a cold bottle of beer in my hand and a hot smooch on my lips. "I'm so proud of you, Del." She smiled, "Now, we can start planning to get married."

Randy's Tavern was full of people just waiting to congratulate us for bringing home the win. Every one of us dropped our heads and looked to the floor. We truly felt humble and did not know how to accept their praise.

Randy chased away the patrons sitting on the stools so we could stay together at the bar and let the girls sit on our laps. He also dropped a dozen coins in the jukebox and played my favorite song, RAGS TO RICHES. It was a new tune by a paisano named Tony Bennett. He could sing the words that spoke to my heart about a guy coming up poor, but wanting so much more.

Free drinks flowed and some of us actually ate the overpriced sandwiches and potato salad brought in from Hans' delicatessen. My song played over and over until our throats were hoarse from singing and cheering.

The whole night was a dream come true filled with fun and camaraderie. We promised to stay close, no matter where our lives took us. When it came time for the ladies to go home, the team wanted to stay together for a little while longer. Begging off from our usual escort duty, we asked our sweethearts if we could stay with the team on such a special night.

"After all," Mike told his girl, "it's our last time together in uniform."

The ladies understood. We kissed them goodbye and paid for their cab rides.

Rehashing the game for the next hour, we savored every play. Close to midnight, when it was just us at the bar with our sponsor, Randy pulled out our envelopes. Ripping them open, we were surprised to see twice the money we had expected. A thousand bucks could go a long way toward building our futures and we were extremely grateful.

"You boys deserve it," Randy winked, "I had a great run this season with you guys out there hustling for the tavern. Sure wish you'd play another year?"

Eddy Dee spoke for all of us. "Nah, we're getting too old. This is a young man's game and besides, we're tired of the bull crap." We all nodded in agreement. "Thanks again for the extra money."

Every team member added his reason why it was time to hang up his uniform and move on to an adult life. It wasn't the first time Randy heard we wanted to be city cops or wear the badge in the brand new suburbs popping up. He understood and promised he would help.

Walking out of the tavern, the fellas stopped to search the starry sky and inhale the clean scent of rain coming off the Lake. And for those few last seconds frozen in time, we were still the champions.

As we said our goodbyes, no one had to remind us that we would never be this close again. Our next steps would take us away from our youth and the joy we had shared growing up together.

Bobby waved goodbye and ducked around the corner.

Lou, Mike and the Harrison boys headed down the sidewalk.

Teddy and I stood beside Eddy Dee to cross Belmont Avenue.

We didn't have both feet off the curb when a dark sedan, parked in the shadows to our left, fired up its engine. Hidden back from the street lights, it caught us by surprise. Hesitating, we waited for its headlights that never showed.

The dark car leapt forward and accelerated, coming right at us. Before we could step back on the sidewalk, the blur of a speeding car smashed against all three of us. Our bodies flew back to the tavern's brick wall.

I saw stars even when Bobby pulled me to my feet. We yelled curses at the bastards' brake lights, but the car sped through the intersection heading west. Teddy turned to me and we both knew who was behind the wheel.

Randy's voice yelled from the door, "I called the cops. An ambulance is on the way." When we turned around, I realized why Randy said the word, ambulance. Eddy hadn't gotten up off the sidewalk with us. His limp body was still pushed up against the building and he did not look good.

Teddy and I followed the ambulance to the hospital and found Eddy still passed out in the emergency room. He never woke up and died of massive internal injuries at sunrise. Doctors tried to explain why he did not make it while we both survived with bruises. None of it made sense and fired up our anger even more.

The coppers went to Nunzio's house, but found out he was hiding at his grandmother's place. Sure enough his black car had a passenger-side broken headlight along with all kinds of dents. He told the cops that his car had been stolen. It took two hours for them to beat the bloody truth out of him. Still, he was only charged with hit and run along with vehicular manslaughter.

Eddy's funeral was huge. The whole neighborhood turned out to pay their respects. I cringed as the funeral procession approached St. Joseph's tall iron gates. And according to its tradition, the bell tolled to announce that Eddy had come to his final resting place.

It was awful. We all sobbed. I'll never forget looking at that six-foot hole in the ground while we were still struggling to believe that Eddy was really dead. When we drove away, I felt a six-foot hole in my heart.

The trial was a joke. Although we begged the state's attorney for a first degree murder charge, Eddy's killer received a paltry few years probation. And when justice wasn't served, we accepted the part we were meant to play because by then Bobby, Teddy and me were on the city force. We planned to behave while we were rookies, but after that we were determined to keep a close eye on Nunzio.

Within the year, Randy pulled strings with our alderman and brought us right back to the neighborhood police station. There was something strangely wicked in Randy's eyes when he said, "I made sure our champions are patrolling our streets and watching over certain felons enjoying probation out there."

RED AND WHITE

By Kalyani Kurup

'Red and white, ready to fight', is a limerick that I had often chanted when I was a child. The words do ring true because red and white are indeed contrasting colors. But the equation changed for me later, and I now think of red and white as hues of harmony.

The incident that changed my mind occurred on the day I saw snow for the first time.

Till then I was acquainted with snow only through the images that photographers froze, and the words that poets let loose. I was told that snow is soundless, that snowfall is the most silent form of movement in the natural world. But curiously enough, my introduction to snow was through its sound, and not through its silence.

I was living in a village in a Himalayan valley then, and it was the first winter after we had relocated there. The day before that first snowfall, it was raining almost the whole day but by the time it became night, the sound of rain had stopped.

In the morning I woke up to the sound of thuds outside. I was alone at home and I felt a bit frightened because in that semi-conscious state between wakefulness and sleep, I thought that someone was banging on the door.

I got up and cautiously looked out of the upper story window to find out where the sound was coming from.

What I saw in front of me took my breath away.

It had probably snowed the whole of the previous night, because, there in front of me was an incredible ocean of shimmering whiteness. There was not a single blade of grass, or blossom on the bush, or bit of a boulder, that was not covered with snow. Just the previous evening, the earth was a rich palette of colors. But now the whole world was just one color – a dazzling white. It was an incredibly beautiful sight.

And the thuds continued. I realized that it was the sound of large lumps of snow sliding down the sloping roofs and falling to the ground.

I swathed myself in layers of woolens and went to the gate to explore. A yak came ambling down the road. I wondered about nature's judgment which made that animal so compliant to the climate but made man dependent on sweaters, snow-boots and sou'westers to survive.

As I stood there mulling over nature's idiosyncrasies, I saw a small red ball on the white hill opposite. It looked like a single big cherry that the snow had forgotten to shroud. I wondered how the snow could have forgotten to cover that one cherry, while it had covered all those gigantic mountain ranges around.

Then, to my surprise, I found that the cherry was moving. It was rolling down the hill, albeit quite slowly.

As the cherry rolled down slowly, it became larger and larger, and soon I realized that it was a man.

The cherry that turned into a man as it rolled down was actually a lama walking down the hill. His monastery was probably somewhere behind that hill. It was his red robe that had made him look like a cherry to me from a distance.

When he finally reached the road that passed in front of my house, I found that he was not wearing a sweater or a cap. He was wearing the same maroon robe that he wore in the summer. He seemed more attuned to the cold than even that yak.

"Don't you feel cold, sir?" I asked him.

"No," he said, smiling. And he pointed at the yak. "Does this animal feel cold?" he asked. "When you live in harmony with nature, you become used to its changes. Only those who have moved away from nature feel hot or cold."

He seemed to be a man who had merged with nature in body and in spirit. I raised my joined palms to him in salutation.

I stood watching as he walked past. As he moved further and further away, he became smaller and smaller and finally he once again became the cherry that he was at first. Then he completely vanished into the snow, as a stunning visual image of man merging completely with nature. They became one, the way a body and a soul fuse into one, the way light vanishes into darkness at night, and darkness vanishes into light at dawn.

128

The sheer beauty of that sight was enough to make it unforgettable forever. However, there was also a sequel to the incident that burned the memory of that morning forever in my mind although in a slightly unpleasant way.

A few years after it happened, I narrated the incident as one of my Toastmasters club speeches. It was a project for which we were expected to paint "vivid images with words," and to use rhetorical devices such as similes and alliterations and triads. My description of the red lama merging into the white snow, and usages like "red and white as hues of harmony," "blade of grass, or blossom on the bush, or bit of a boulder," and "sweaters, snow-boots and sou'westers to survive," etc. fully satisfied the requirements of the project. My fellow Toastmasters appreciated the speech very much.

Since my club members liked it, when our club conducted a speechcraft course for the employees of a multinational, they asked me to give the speech as a sample of a Toastmaster project. There too, everyone admired the descriptive speech so that rightly or wrongly I became convinced that it was indeed a wonderful speech.

A couple of years later, I became a member of another Toastmasters club in another country. I was in India the first time, but in 2009 I happened to be in the USA and joined a Toastmasters club in the new country.

During one of the meetings, there was a shortage of speakers and the master of ceremonies asked if someone could speak to fill the gap. I volunteered because I remembered the speech about the snow and the lama so clearly that I had no problem giving it off the cuff.

I was given a slot and when my turn came I went to the lectern and started narrating my favorite story of a single cherry dotting the dazzling white world of snowbound Himalayan ranges.

However, halfway into the speech I noticed that there was a blank expression on the listeners' faces. I continued with the speech nevertheless, but when I was narrating my conversation with the lama, most of them looked at me as if I was off my rocker.

I stopped and asked my audience whether they were following what I was saying. No one gave a clear-cut answer.

I wondered where I could have gone wrong in my description. There were only two characters in my story – the snow-clad mountains and the red-robed lama. First I thought that maybe my description of snow was not good enough. But that did not make much sense because it was unlikely that anyone would have difficulty in imagining snow-covered Himalayan ranges.

Then there was my second character – the lama.

"I hope you know who a lama is," I said hesitantly.

"Oh, yes," someone said. "It is more or less camel-like and its meat…"

You could have knocked me down with a feather! A lama is a meat animal? For me, as for many in Asia, a lama is the representative of the beautiful, peaceful Buddhist religion.

Of course, my shock was only momentary. I understood instantly. None of my audience had probably seen a Buddhist lama. A lama, for them, was 'llama', the South American pack animal with banana-shaped ears and a short tail – an animal that is killed for meat. No wonder they were staring at me as if I was half-gaga when I spoke about a llama that was the color of blood, rolled down a hill, and later conversed with me.

Phonetically, lama and llama are the same. Worse, nowadays there is even a genus of llamas spelt as lama.

One of the cardinal rules of good speaking, as taught in the Toastmasters club, is that a speaker should tailor his speech precisely to suit the interests and comprehension criteria of the audience. In fact, in one my Toastmasters club projects I had given an elaborate presentation on how a speaker should do some research on the background and interests of the audience before preparing a speech.

I had failed miserably in molding my speech to fit the listeners' understanding. I felt like someone who had fallen into a bucket of tar. Though I did give them a short description of the religious lama as different from the meat animal llama, I did not feel like continuing the speech.

I did complete it though, because it was not proper to walk back to your seat in the middle of a speech. I finished it and returned to my seat like a burst balloon.

With that fiasco, the lama and the snow became doubly unforgettable to me.

TEENAGE UNWISDOM

By Edgar Brown

The years between 1940 and 1947 were the happiest years of my life. Like many teenagers approaching maturity, I found my spirits soaring one minute and plummeting the next—a gamut one must run along the road to adulthood. I was a good student in high school, but I had difficulty with math and flunked plane geometry my senior year—there was nothing plain about geometry to me! Instead of graduating in the spring, I had to go to summer school in order to finish.

In the pre-dawn hours of a Sunday in 1946, I was delivering newspapers in Austin, Texas, when I met Nick Webster, who was delivering papers on an adjoining route. We were both carrying bags over our shoulders, folding the papers as we walked along and tossing them on lawns and porches. I had seen him at high school, but he wasn't in any of my classes and we hadn't spent any time together. Both of us welcomed company and decided to walk our Sunday routes together, a practice we continued thereafter. As we became better acquainted, we found much in common and enjoyed being together.

We met each other's families. Nick's father was editor of the Texas Eastern Star, a Masonic magazine published in Austin. He, his wife Lois, her sister Daisy and Nick's brother Grady lived in Hemphill Park, just a few blocks from Pearl Street where I lived. Daisy's husband Oscar was a prisoner of war of the Japanese on the Island of Java. (When Oscar returned after the war, Nick and I spent a lot of time with him and Daisy at their ranch in the hills west of Austin.) My father was teaching ancient history at the University of Texas. In 1947, we moved to California after he accepted an offer to teach at U.C.L.A.

Nick's parents bought 80 acres of land near Oak Hill, a small town southwest of Austin, where they planned to build a house. The land was undeveloped. Cedar trees covered the property from the dirt road at one end to a distinctive hill at the other. There was no fence or

131

any other structure on the premises, and no water. From all that appeared, the land had never been occupied.

The Websters had built a fence and dug a well long before I visited what they came to call the "Place." By the time I began accompanying Nick and his parents to the Place, they had already built a garage and had moved into it. They invited me to stay there during summer school, and my parents allowed me to do so. Nick was also going to summer school, which made this arrangement convenient for both of us.

Nick and I had a number of chores, including milking the cow, cultivating a small orchard, and helping his father quarry rock for the new house. An abundance of limestone layers close to the surface of the ground supplied ample stone for construction of the house. Nick, his father and I spent much of our time digging out the limestone layers and cutting them into small enough pieces for the workmen to lift.

The Websters hired two or three Mexicans to do the rock work on the house. They proved to be fine masons, truly artists in their choice and arrangement of the stones. In fact, their conferring at length about which stone to place in what part of the wall became somewhat disconcerting to Nick's father, who was paying them by the hour.

On our journeys back and forth to the Place, Nick's mother taught me how to drive, and I soon obtained a license. This made it easier for us to come and go to school. We also cleared land for the orchard by cutting down the small cedar trees and pulling out the roots with an old tractor Nick's father bought for this purpose. We enjoyed lighting huge bonfires to dispose of the debris.

One day Nick drove to Round Rock, a few miles north of Austin, where he visited an antique store. He took a fancy to and bought an old Army rifle complete with cartridges and a bayonet. Upon examining it, we found it to be a .45 Caliber, 1870 Springfield rifle. The lead bullets had been removed from the cartridges and replaced with paper wadding. We were excited about the gun and talked of little else as we did our chores that evening. We fantasized about using the rifle in some kind of theatrical production. This led us to think of using the rifle in a skit on parents' night at the Tom Wooten Scout Camp. We began making up a skit to perform at the scout camp.

Nick, Grady and I were members of Troop 10, which met once a week at the Pease Elementary School near the university campus. I always looked forward to meetings. We sang scout songs and played all kinds of games on the playground and in the halls of the school. They were mostly running games, like Capture the Flag. Some of the leaders of Troop 10 were college students. We looked up to them and benefited from their experience. Other scout troops in the area were more formal and controlled than we were. To them I'm sure Troop 10 looked more like a mob than a scout troop.

World War ll brought changes. Most of our leaders went into one of the military services, and we began to work on projects to help in the war effort. One, for example, was to meet on Saturday mornings and collect newspapers from Austin neighborhoods. This proved to be a boon to the troop, which received money for the paper. Another project was to train to do military things, such as learning the Morse code, practicing first aid, and working out to become physically fit.

Camp Wooten occupies a high bluff overlooking Bull Creek and the Colorado River. It is a haven for scout troops in central Texas. Summer sees a succession of scout troops coming and going to Camp Wooten, which is about 7 miles from Austin. I had been there several times myself, and when I was there last I served as Camp Bugler. One of the highlights each week is parents' night. Families with scouts at the camp come to a special campfire in a large arena where they sit on logs around the fire. Scouts from the various troops provide the entertainment. Actors often enter and exit the circle a number of times, like acts in a play, to develop their stories. This is how Nick and I envisioned performing our skit.

Parents' night was only a few days away. We obtained permission to put on our skit, which we perfected each night after we finished our chores. It occurred to us that we should try out the rifle to make sure it was still in working order. We brought the rifle out after dark, loaded it with one of the shells and fired toward the woods. There was a loud bang; flame shot out of the barrel and Nick, who fired the shot, jerked back from the kick. We were thrilled to find the rifle was in working order. It didn't occur to us to check to see whether it hit anything. We were in a state of total denial. We closed our minds to anything that might jeopardize our plan. Except for deciding who would do the shooting, we were ready to go.

We planned to stay in town after school and go directly to Camp Wooten. Nick brought the rifle to school to show our friends. In those days it was common to see someone board a city bus carrying a firearm. One had only to show the driver the gun was not loaded before taking a seat. Nevertheless, we attracted a lot of attention at school and enjoyed a brief moment of celebrity. The teachers were unhappy to see the rifle, but they didn't ask us to leave. After school, Nick and I went to pick up my older sister, Pat, who wanted to go with us.

It was almost dark when we reached Camp Wooten. There was an air of excitement as parents and friends poured into the arena. A large campfire lit up their faces as they sat on logs around the circle. Nick and I went over our skit one more time. Nick was to be the shooter. He and I were to enter from opposite sides of the circle. I was to call him names and insult him. We would then exit the circle and, sometime later, repeat the scene. In the final scene, Nick was to enter with the rifle and a bucket of water. He was to shoot me, throw the bucket of water over me and drag me out of the arena.

The first two scenes caught on with the audience, which looked forward to the next act. Nick and I confronted each other in the last scene. When he started to raise the rifle, I became very nervous and walked to another part of the circle, turned and slowly walked back to my place. I had never had him point the rifle at me before and suddenly found myself very anxious. He fired the rifle. The first thing I realized was that I didn't need to fall; the impact of the shot had already knocked me down. As Nick approached with the bucket of water, I told him through clenched teeth to get me out of there. Nick immediately realized something was wrong and quickly dragged me out. No one in the audience realized there had been an accident.

Outside the arena, I lay on the ground. I was not in pain, but there was blood from a large lump on my jaw, and my chest and stomach felt numb. My sister Pat arrived, quickly assessed the situation and had someone call an ambulance. I reached Seaton Hospital in Austin about 45 minutes later. I was very upset when I realized I was being taken to the operating room because I didn't yet understand that I had been struck with lead pellets. Nick and I thought I had been struck with paper wadding. The cartridges, it turned out, had been loaded with bird shot; the paper wadding merely held the lead pellets in place.

The surgeon labored for five hours picking through my small intestines to remove lead pellets. Some of the pellets had even exited my back. Thanks to a good surgeon, penicillin and a truck load of soldiers from Camp Swift who volunteered to give blood, I made a full recovery. I still carry a number of pellets in my body. When I awoke after the surgery, the doctor was standing at the foot of my bed. He told me I should be thankful to be alive and that if I was not already going to church, I should start attending..

I told Nick he should be thankful I wasn't the shooter. There is almost no chance that another shot would have missed so many vital organs. This is just further proof, in my case dramatic proof, of the time lag between physical maturity and judgment.

THE WAGON RACE

By Edgar Brown

I'll never forget the spring of 1936. I was in the third grade at the Highland School in Boulder, Colorado. It was two weeks before summer vacation, which the school celebrated with a Field Day. On Field Day the whole school, including parents and siblings, gathered on the playground to watch all manner of competitions: foot races, long jumps, high jumps, and for me the most exciting of all, the wagon race.

The wagon race required teams of two persons, one to push the other to the turnaround point, change places and race back to the starting line. I became obsessed with the wagon race—it was an opportunity to win a blue ribbon and to impress my parents and friends. I was confident I could win if I had the right partner.

This brings me to Wayne, one of the strongest boys in my class. He was my size, which would give us an advantage over teams in which one rider was bigger than the other. At recess on the day the school announced Field Day, I went straight up to Wayne on the playground and asked him to be my partner. I was worried that he would team up with someone else. We were not best friends, but Wayne and I had gotten along fairly well. I was thrilled when he agreed and especially because he was just as excited about the race as I was.

Wayne and I decided to practice at recess every day before Field Day. Since I lived only a few blocks from school and had a good wagon, I began bringing it every day. Other teams brought their wagons too. We spent recesses pushing each other from one end of the playground to the other. It became apparent to us, and probably to the other teams, that we were by far the fastest. Wayne and I knew we would take the ribbon. I told my parents we would win and invited them to be there.

Time passed quickly, and we found ourselves at the starting line on Field Day. A teacher reviewed the route for the wagon race. Wayne and I didn't need to hear about the route—we had been practicing all week and knew the route. We anxiously waited for the red flag to start the race.

The teacher waved the flag. Wayne and I along with the other teams jumped forward; the race was on. I steered and Wayne pushed. Within seconds we were in the lead. Wayne pushed as hard as he could until we felt almost alone on the field. When we reached the other side of the playground, I jumped out of the wagon and Wayne jumped in as we turned for the finish line. To our horror and amazement we saw that the other teams had already finished—they had turned around half way across the playground. As I pushed the wagon toward the finish line, we passed a white line which we now realized was the official turnaround line. I pushed the wagon to a last place finish.

That was many, many years ago, but it still hurts.

WALLS

By Hannah Grace Stanton

Like many adults who are now of a certain age, I grew up hearing my father proclaim "children should be seen and not heard." Maybe he received the same admonition when he was a child. Following his advice, and wanting to be loved by him, I learned early on to keep my feelings hidden and my thoughts to myself.

My mother was a stay-at-home mom, but I mostly remember her as a stay-at-home-passed-out-in-the-bed mom. Her pattern was to get drunk in the evenings, fight with my father and sleep it off the next day. She became violent when she drank. It was not unusual for her to chase my father up the stairs and literally tear the shirt off his back. I never saw my father hit my mother, although I often saw him holding her wrists to keep her from hitting him. In retrospect, I understand that my mother was numbing her own pain, a side effect of which was to further numb me emotionally.

With Mom sleeping and Dad at work, I was often alone during my preschool years. Fortunately we had Siamese cats to fill the void at home. Being Siamese, they were very vocal and made for good company. The need that I later developed to always have a cat in my life had its origin in the comfort that these cats provided me.

The cats also served as a connection between my parents and me. My mother loved cats, and, although he wasn't demonstrative about it, my father appeared to enjoy them as well.

My favorite among all of my cats was a Seal Point Siamese that I named Wooley. I had gotten him as a kitten when I was nine or ten years old. Wooley was a classic Apple-head Siamese with a cream-colored body and dark brown face, tail, legs, and paws. He had brilliant blue, slightly crossed eyes and a characteristic guttural meow. Wooley was affectionate, which delighted me, as well as extremely intelligent. My mother trained him, by coaxing him with food, to sit upright in her palm on his hind legs. He even learned to use the toilet and would run ahead of anyone whom he saw approaching a bathroom so that he could show off his self-taught talent.

Wooley, like all cats, was curious. If a door was ajar he hooked it with his paw so he could pull it open to see what was on the other side. He was especially adept at opening the sliding doors that separated the living room from the dining room. One door in the house — the attic door — couldn't be shut tightly because the doorknob had fallen apart. I did my best to keep our cats out of the attic because there was a large hole in the wall where some of the plasterboard had come loose. One Saturday afternoon, Wooley discovered he could pry open the door without much effort and, unnoticed, ran up the stairs to explore.

* * *

I was in my bedroom reading when I heard Wooley begin to yowl. His cries seemed to be coming from my father's office. Wooley sounded distressed, so I rushed to the room and began looking for him. I checked the supply closet as well as behind and beneath my father's large steel desk. I then went to look behind the glass-paned bookcase, thinking he might be trapped in an avalanche of magazines. I pressed the side of my face against the wall to get a better view. He wasn't there, but I noticed that the closer I was to the wall, the louder he sounded.

I walked to the adjoining room and scanned the floor. Wooley wasn't by the toilet or under the sink. I dropped to my hands and knees and looked under the cast-iron clawfoot tub. I continued calling him and, hearing me, his howls grew louder and more distressed. Following the sound of his cries, I opened the small built-in closet that was near the bathtub. It was then that I realized Wooley was on the other side of the closet. He had gotten into the attic, found the hole in the wall, and fallen into it. There was no way that I could get to him. I was helpless, and my beloved cat was going to die a horrible death entombed within the walls of the house.

It being a Saturday, my father was at home. I ran to him and told him about Wooley. (I don't remember my mother being at home at the time.) While Dad went to the basement for tools, I emptied the closet. My father returned with a claw hammer and wedge, stepped into the tub, and began loosening the boards in the closet. We worked as a team, him handing me the boards as he removed them. After what felt like an eternity, but was probably only ten minutes, Dad created a hole large enough for him to reach in and retrieve a screaming and very dusty cat. My father was my hero that day, and fifty years later I continue to be in awe of how he flew into action to rescue Wooley. I wish he could have been a different kind of father, though, and known how to tear through my walls to rescue me when I fell.

It was easy to resolve never to drink or use drugs after having seen what it did to my mother. My first night at college, however, I went to a party and came back to the dorm so drunk that I had bruises from having fallen several times while staggering up the stairs. Neither the next day's hangover nor the bruises deterred me from doing it all over again the next night, and the next, and soon I was drinking every day.

The night before Thanksgiving break I had been drinking, became depressed, and took several Librium. I have no recollection of getting there, but I woke to find myself in the college infirmary with a grumpy nurse hovering over me threatening to pump my stomach. I spent the rest of the night in the infirmary and was released from there into my father's care the following morning. Neither my father nor I mentioned anything about the incident during the two-hour drive home or any time thereafter.

By my sophomore year in college, I discovered that drugs removed me from myself quite effectively, and more quickly than alcohol. I had found a reliable source from which I could get anything I wanted — pot, acid, amphetamines. Amphetamines were among my favorites because they made me feel so powerful. One weekend when I was at home, I noticed my father's pills in the kitchen cabinet. I discovered he had a prescription for a weight-loss drug, the capsules of which were identical to those I purchased on the street. I stole a few of the pills whenever I had the opportunity. He never noticed they were missing.

The last time I stole pills from my father he caught me. The prescription had recently been refilled, and I was like the kid in the candy store. I took about a third of the capsules and hid them in a Styrofoam owl that I had hollowed out for stashing drugs. That evening I heard my father in his bedroom pour out the pills and count them, dropping them one by one back into the plastic vial. My heart pounded as I listened to him dump them out and count them a second time. As he and I were the only ones in the house, it would be obvious who had stolen his pills. I didn't know what was worse — being found out as a thief or being a disappointment to my father. I never knew because he never said a word about the pills. At the time I was relieved but looking back, and knowing what I know now, my father's failure to ask me about the missing pills left me feeling unnoticed and that I didn't matter to him.

I continued drinking and using drugs throughout college. My grades fluctuated from Dean's List to average, which is probably why I was able to graduate despite failing five classes one quarter because I never completed the coursework. The college sent my grades to my father each quarter, and I saw where he had opened the envelope. He never asked me about the five Fs.

Upon graduating I moved away from home. While I was at college, my father had taken our three Siamese — including Wooley — and had them euthanized because he traveled two or three days a week on work and was unable to take care of them. I didn't know he had planned on doing this, and I never had a chance to say goodbye to them.

After settling into my new apartment, one of the first things I did was adopt a homeless kitten that I named Star. I continued to drink and struggle with depression but kept it to myself. I credit Star with saving my life: one night when I was depressed, and writing a note, I realized I had no one whom I could trust to take care of him. My need to provide a safe home for him outweighed my need to escape the pain of my life.

In retrospect, I learned something about parenting that evening: I needed to make it through my own pain so that I could take care of this cat that I had brought into my life. My mother had been unable, or not strong enough, to face her pain and she abandoned me time and again, choosing the comfort of drink. Perhaps my father never confronted me about my self-destructiveness because it would have hurt too deeply to realize his daughter was traveling the same path as his wife.

Both my parents are now dead. My father was a good man, and I admire many things about him. My mother would have been so different if she had been able to get sober, as I am today. Although my parents were not perfect, they were *my* parents and growing up in their household led me to seek therapy as an adult. For that I thank them. Over the years, I have learned to navigate a world of feelings through which my parents could only stumble. It has been a slow journey, undoing what I learned as a child, and sometimes I still find it difficult to allow myself to be heard or to believe anyone wants to hear what I have to say. Of one thing I am certain: words — whether spoken, heard, or written — are among the most effective tools for breaking down walls.

WHAT I DID FOR LOVE

By Sunny Hersh

Men's clothes are boring, aren't they? As the shirts whirled around on the dry cleaner's conveyer, I noticed a pattern – light blue, white, light blue, white, blue-and-white stripes, white, light blue, dark blue. Every once in a while you might see a pale yellow or a grey stripe. The clerk went right past my husband's shirts, but I saw them clearly from across the shop. Navy blue check, multicolored red plaid, purple, pink, black, aqua with white stripes – the colorful shirts refused to be smothered by their boring brethren. Smiling, but with tears in my eyes, I remembered why I hopped in a cab and drove away from everything I knew 42 years ago to be with the man who wears those shirts.

"This is Scott, he eats in my cafeteria," said my girlfriend Kathy as we passed Halloween revelers hiking up the hill to MemAud, the aging theater on the Ohio University green. It was 1970 and the air was filled with the smell of marijuana as we pretended to enjoy three artsy short horror films. Scott seemed nice enough, didn't say much, and was as shocked as we were when the driver of the sexy convertible had his head cut off at a road block at the end of the last film.

"Hmm, Scott must be a rich kid," I thought when we stopped in his dorm room on the way back from the movie and looked at the beautiful photographs he'd taken on a graduation trip to Europe. That used to be me. These days, though, I was hanging by a financial thread, working in a go-go bar on campus to buy books and pizza. All hell had broken loose in my family since my father's car dealership went bankrupt, my parents moved to Florida to escape creditors, and my father had a stroke that paralyzed the right side of his body.

Months later I came back to school a week early from Christmas break, so happy to get away from the bitter sadness that filled the air in my parent's home. I saw Scott again at a New Year's party in someone's dorm room, complete with Black Sabbath, black light, and fluorescent posters. He kept sitting down next to me and seemed to want to say something as I circulated around the room. When he finally asked me if I wanted to go to a fraternity party with him, I told him I would but…I was seeing someone.

That was only half true. I'd been hanging out with George and a hilarious group of guys from Cleveland that I met the first day on campus. Their idea of a good time was to poop in a shoe box, gift wrap the box, leave it in front of someone's dorm room, and loiter in the hall to hear the reaction. Since I was the biggest Honor Society, editor-of-the-high-school-newspaper, goody two-shoes Dork who ever lived, I thought this was not only funny but cool, and I traded a few kisses with George for the privilege of being the group's mascot.

Apparently George's girlfriend in Cleveland got wind of those kisses. The day after that New Year's party, George showed me where she'd put out a cigarette on his forearm. We agreed that our budding relationship had been nipped and said goodbye.

Meanwhile, Scott launched his future as a salesman by inviting my friend Kathy to the fraternity party. His goal, he said later, was to go out with me, but he was using an old salesman's trick – the takeaway. And sure enough, I felt a little deflated and called Kathy a week after their date.

"So Kath…uh…how are you feeling about that Scott guy? Are you into him or would it be okay if I called him?"

"Sure, go ahead," she said. "We didn't really get it on or anything." (Yeah, we really used to talk that way.) Coming from Kathy, that really meant something, 'cause she was a notorious nympho around the quad.

Kathy told him I was interested, and one night there was a knock on my window. The women's dorms still had a curfew and it was after curfew, but there was Scott, standing on a chair. We talked happily about nothing for an hour with our elbows on the windowsill until a security guard came by, tapped Scott on the knee cap, and said "Lemme see yer ID, son."

The next night he walked me to my job at the go-go bar and escorted me back to the dorm when the bar closed at 1 a.m. We were together every possible minute from that day forward, and our names became one name, as in Sunny-and-Scott. Friends never saw one without the other or said one without the other…until the end of spring semester.

144

The public phone hung on the wall in the dorm's hallway in those days. If your room was near the phone, you knew who was going out, who was breaking up, and who was heading to Canada for an abortion. My time to call home was Sunday about 4, and one bright April day my parents told me they couldn't afford to send me back to school in the fall. Truth be told, they didn't see why I needed a college degree and hoped I'd become a dental assistant. I packed up my stuff, folded my perfect academic record into my pocket, and cried all the way to West Palm Beach.

Scott and I had a plan – we would both work as hard as we could to come up with $4,000 for a year's tuition so I could come back to school. Scott talked his parents into paying him to paint their house. I sold lingerie in a department store during the day and seated patrons in a high-priced steak house at night. With minimum wage at about $1.60 an hour, well….you do the math. But we were game.

I remember standing on one foot in the restaurant's bathroom stall, wiggling into my short little hostess dress and talking to a waitress washing her hands. "Why are so many of our customers men and why are they all named Smith and Johnson?" I asked her.

She was still laughing when she left the bathroom and all the waitresses were cackling and staring at me when I came out. One took pity on me and took me aside, explaining that our restaurant was known as a popular place for gay men to bring their dates. I nodded and said thank you, but had no idea what that meant. I mean, I was a 19-year-old Midwesterner, you know?

"Randy," I asked my older brother, "what's a gay man?" He smiled and leaned in, whispering "That's men who like to have sex with men."

"Ohhh," I said, confused. "And how does that work?"

"Geez," he laughed, "don't you know? They're butt buddies!" I kind of got it, but all I really needed to know is that these nicely groomed men were very kind and they were excellent tippers. I kept my money in an envelope in my parent's home safe, counting it every week and dreaming of being back at school with Scott.

We boomers are probably the last generation to write love letters and send them in the mail. Scott's were so sweet, filled with lists of all the fun things we'd do when we were back together. And I mean ALL the fun things! On my day off, I'd be first at the mailbox but Mom brought in the mail most days. Apparently she'd been opening my letters, reading them, and then sealing them back up again.

Our notes of love, lust and dreams for the future had my parents simmering with anger, erupting into a full boil when Scott came for a visit and stayed in our guest room. After about two days of polite silence, a screaming fight began. The issue that put them over the edge was my intention to convert to Judaism. I'd fallen in love with the ancient traditions and intellectual freedom of Judaism as I'd fallen in love with Scott.

"Am I supposed to be happy that you two are having sex and she wants to be a Jew like you?!" my father screamed, backing Scott into a corner and raising his arm.

I knew Dad was capable of violence, had experienced it myself, and yanked Scott out of there, called a cab and helped him pack his stuff and head back to the airport. I saved up my tip quarters to call him from the payphone at work and kept saving money, frightened by my parent's anger but working literally day and night to return to school.

One day I discovered that most of the money was missing from my envelope. I don't remember if I was angry, hurt or both – how could my parents take my money without asking me? Were their money problems really that bad? But it was evident that Scott and I needed a new plan. He raided his house-painting money and found me a place to live on campus. Our plan was for me to work and save money while living in our college town, establishing in-state residency and lowering my future tuition costs. He sent my plane ticket to a friend at work.

The day of my exodus arrived. Wearing my hostess dress, I told my parents I was leaving for work and parked my mom's car around the corner, waiting for them to head out for dinner with friends. The cab for the airport showed up minutes later, waiting while I threw everything I could fit into my blue camper trunk. My brain was on fire, filled with excitement and a sense of purpose. I can still picture the chubby cab driver obligingly sitting on the trunk so I could close it.

The note to my parents said, "You know where I've gone. I won't be in touch for a while." I don't remember whether I signed it 'love' or not, but I knew I was drawing a line in the sand between girl and woman.

146

ABOUT THE AUTHORS

F. CLIFTON BERRY, JR. writes articles and books—and has edited magazines—on defense and aerospace topics. He has flown as a private pilot, single-engine land and sea. He also jumped out of airplanes during his career as an airborne Infantry officer in the US Army.

EDGAR BROWN is a retired attorney who was employed by the Justice Department from 1963 to 2007.

MARY ELLEN GAVIN is a writer ... literary editor ... script consultant.

SUNNY HERSH is the author of two books celebrating life after 40 -- *Midlife Mamas on the Moon* and *Is it HOT in here or am I just HOT!* A new resident of northern Virginia, she's currently writing women's fiction that will give you some giggle with your sizzle. She's been married to Scott for 40 years.

DIANE HUNTER has enjoyed sharing her short stories in the WOC anthologies for the past 8 years. It has been a life-long dream of hers to write about the people she loves most—her family. Her unforgettable story is a tribute to her husband, Reuben.

DENICE JOBE'S features and essays have appeared in *The Washington Post* and *Chicken Soup for the Soul: Twins and More*, among others. She lives in Centreville, Virginia,with her husband, Steve, and twin boys, Nick and Henry. www.denicealdrichjobe.com

PATRICIA BOSWELL KALLMAN is an award-winning writer, director and producer in theatre and television. She is a co-founder of The Alliance Theatre in Virginia. Pat and husband, Roy, are proud parents of two daughters.

RICHARD KATCHMARK works a day job to feed the family. He writes so that ideas and words inside him can have life on paper. He can't keep his mind shut. Six book-length writings (two nonfiction and four fiction) plus four booklets of snippets have received life.

DANA KING has published two e-books, *Wild Bill* and *Worst Enemies*. *Grind Joint*, the second book in the series begun by *Worst Enemies*, will be published in paper by Stark House in 2014. His short fiction has appeared in Thuglit, Powder Burn Flash, New Mystery Reader, and Mysterical-E, as well as the anthology, *Blood, Guts, and Whisky*. He lives in Maryland with his Beloved Spouse and does not like to be disturbed while reading.

KALYANI KURUP For more works of the writer, please see https://www.amazon.com/author/kalyanikurup

J.J. LENART lives with his wife near Charlotte, North Carolina; is the parent of five tax-paying adults, and the ready-and-willing conspirator to a posse of seven grandchildren. He is a former cartographer, and enjoys storytelling and writes predominantly adventure thrillers.

RUTH PERRY is a retired long term health care administrator, social worker, wife, mother and grandmother of six grandchildren and community volunteer. She is a lifelong student and takes classes at OLLI (Osher Life Long Leaning Institute) on the George Mason University Campus. Ruth and her husband live in Fairfax, Virginia. She is currently working on a children's book.

HANNAH GRACE STANTON is the pen name of a member of The Writers of Chantilly. Inspired by Jeannette Walls' *The Glass Castle*, she is working on a memoir of overcoming the destructive forces that influenced her early life. The least productive member of WOC, Stanton appreciates the group's patience and acceptance of her as she grows into the writer she hopes to become.

JOHN C. STIPA is a corporate analyst who loves the beach, woodworking, playing and coaching sports, traveling, good food and storytelling. He is the author of adventure / mystery / romance novels including The Foiled Knight and No Greater Sacrifice. He has also published several short stories with his writing group: The Writers of

Chantilly. Currently, John lives in Virginia with his family working on his next project. Learn more at www.johnstipa.com

MOLLY TEMPLAR is a retired teacher who enjoys writing short stories and poetry. She and her husband live in Virginia and California.

REBECCA THOMPSON was born in Jerusalem, Israel, to Filipino parents. Her father worked for the United Nations taking his family to Europe, Middle East, Asia and Africa. She moved to the U.S. in 1979. Married for over 30 years with two sons, she lives in Virginia. Her passions include gardening, cooking fine cuisine, and interior design. She has been a waitress, Senior Network Support Engineer, Systems/Sales Engineer and assisted in managing a motorcycle rider training company, Motorcycle Riding Concepts. She is currently exploring her next adventure: What to be when she grows up.

PRAYER TISDALE is a student pursuing a degree in business. She loves to sit on her bed, read creative books, and invent creative stories. Her passion is to visit historic sites. From visiting these historic sites and reading her millions of books, she creates stories that will make you weep, laugh, and fantasize.

Made in the USA
San Bernardino, CA
06 December 2013